LEA_ _

TRODDEN

GROUND

ELAINE L. ORR

LEAST TRODDEN GROUND
ELAINE L. ORR

Book 1 of the

Family History Mystery Series

Least Trodden Ground is a work of fiction. All characters and story lines are products of the author's imagination.

elaineorr.com

elaineorr.blogspot.com

DEDICATION

*For Carol Maher Orr. May her memory
live long in our family's history.*

ACKNOWLEDGMENTS

I learned a great deal about my family's history through stories my parents and aunts and uncles told – occasionally with embellishment. Even so, the stories (more than dates and data) gave me an appreciation for history and a desire to learn more. I'm especially grateful to cousins on both sides of the family who also explore – Kathy Seneker Fairchild, Mary Anne Vincent, and Margaret Hauser Pierson. Those experiences gave me the grounding to write this book –– though of course, it's pure fiction! As always, several members of the Decatur Critique Group gave helpful suggestions – especially Angela, Dave, and Sue.

BOOKS IN THE
FAMILY HISTORY MYSTERY SERIES

Least Trodden Ground
Unscheduled Murder Trip
Mountain Rails of Old
Gilded Path to Nowhere

Jolie Gentil Mystery Series
Appraisal for Murder
Rekindling Motives
When the Carny Comes to Town
Any Port in a Storm
Trouble on the Doorstep
Behind the Walls
Vague Images
Ground to a Halt
Holidays in Ocean Alley
The Unexpected Resolution
The Twain Does Meet (novella)
Underground in Ocean Alley
Aunt Madge in the Civil Election (an Aunt Madge story)
Sticky Fingered Books
New Lease on Death
Jolie and Scoobie High School Misadventures (prequel)

River's Edge Series — *set in rural Iowa*
Logland Series — *set in small-town Illinois*

Books are at online retailers, or ask your library or bookstore to order them — in print, large print, ebook and audio. All books have Barnes and Noble editions, which makes them easy to order from those stores.

CHAPTER ONE

THREE PM. ONLY FIFTY minutes until Digger could leave her cubicle and head for home. After an afternoon of so-called contingency planning, she wanted to be away from other people, breathing fresh air. Nothing smelled better than spring in the Appalachian Mountains.

She turned to her computer to pull up a graphic she was working on for Western Maryland Advertising Agency's best client, Mountain Granite Quarry. The quarry had decided to add direct consumer sales of landscaping materials and had come to WMAA to 'pump up' its visibility in the area.

After brainstorming with other staff in the agency, she most liked her friend Holly's suggestion of a heap of tan landscaping rock, with a shovel stuck in the pile, in front of an early 20th-century Victorian home. Digger wadded up an anonymous suggestion that "Mountain Granite Quarry could get its rocks off by delivering pebbles to people." She thought she knew where that one came from.

A knock on her cubicle was accompanied by a question from a man who sat in a cubicle down the hall. In a stage whisper, he asked, "Do you think we'll all be laid off?" No one could accuse forty-something Robert Bingham of a lack of dramatic skills.

Digger eyed him, maintaining calm she didn't totally feel. "I don't think so. A lot of companies cut back because of the virus, but they're either getting back to work or need to let people know they're still open online or whatever. I think we'll get enough work."

"But you had a meeting," Robert began.

"You know the phrase. 'Hope for the best but prepare for the worst.' Management was just looking at options." Digger counted on the layoffs not happening. She'd bought her bungalow in their small town of Maple Grove just six months ago. Mortgages didn't go away with unemployment.

Robert's brow relaxed. "Okay. I'll hold you to that." He turned to head back to his cubicle.

To herself, Digger muttered, "You do that."

She finished a computer drawing of multi-colored bags of small rocks and switched to email. She had requested a day of leave starting ten days from then, to join her Uncle Benjamin on a family history research trips to Washington, DC. They always made it a three-day weekend, one day in the National Archives, one day 'museuming it,' as he said, and at least part of a day with her cousin Franklin. First cousin once removed, since Benjamin was her great uncle. He would correct her.

Leave approved. Digger jotted a note on the electronic office calendar. She smiled thinking about Uncle Benjamin. His dry humor and lack of any pretenses made him easy to be around—though he did get off quite a few zingers. She wished the trip was this weekend.

After she saved the calendar item, she called Uncle Benjamin to tell him the good news.

He answered on the third ring. "Whatever you're selling, I'm not buying."

"How about an original copy of the Declaration of Independence?"

"That you Digger? Caller ID just had an 800 number."

"I'm at work. I…"

"You never call me from your office. Something wrong?"

"Special occasion. My leave got approved for the Friday after the one coming up."

"Humph. You really need permission?"

Digger grinned. "Only if I want to get paid for the time off."

"Ah. Money is good. You coming up here this weekend?"

'Here' was his four-acre property halfway up Meadow Mountain, which he had dubbed the Ancestral Sanctuary. Now that Uncle Benjamin was in his eighties, Franklin had gently urged his father to sell the place and consider moving to the small, but chic, senior condominium complex in Maple Grove. But he said he didn't want to live with a bunch of old people.

"It's supposed to be fifty-five degrees. You want me to start to clear leaves and stuff from the plots behind the house?"

"Maybe, but I've been doing some digging. I think I'll have something to show you."

She knew that Uncle Benjamin wasn't talking about moving earth. He'd hinted a couple times recently that he may have found some new branches in his ever-expanding online family tree. "Are you going to give me any hints?"

"Probably not until after I make you earn them."

"Okay. You know I can figure out anything that has you stumped."

"Respect your elders." He hung up.

"He gets ornerier all the time," she muttered.

Holly spoke from the door to the cubicle. "I take it that was your uncle, not a customer."

"Good assumption. He's insinuated that he has some new family history discovery, but I think he's leading me on. He's explored every physical and online record that relates to the Browning family for three hundred years or more."

Holly plopped in the chair next to Digger's desk and leaned toward her as if about to share a secret. Since her current hairstyle entailed weaving a lot of additional braids into her own cornrows, the braids touched the desk. "I'm hearing rumors of layoffs, or at least furloughs."

"Have you been talking to Robert?"

"Oh, does he know?"

Digger shook her head, only half in frustration. "No one *knows*. The company's developing a lot of new signage for social distancing and stuff. That'll keep some people busy."

Holly sat back in her chair. "I hope it's not true. Unemployment wouldn't cover half of my bills." She met Digger's gaze. "Would your uncle help you out?"

"He...might, but I wouldn't ask." As carefully as Uncle Benjamin guarded his money, she wasn't about to be in his debt. Maybe if she got sick or something.

"My grandmother is on the Maple Grove Historical Society Board with him. I guess you know some people are still put out about him sort of forcing a move from the old train depot into the two buildings on the square."

Digger's eyebrows went up. "The train depot's pretty much falling apart. I thought any hard feelings were over after everything was moved in and they had that party."

Holly shrugged. "I don't know all the ins and outs. I guess it costs more or something. Utilities, maybe."

"Jeez. I hope they don't ask him for a bigger donation. I'll have to hear about it on our drive to DC next week."

"I think they're raising the dues, applying for a grant or something."

"Ouch," Digger said. "Now shoo. I have stuff to do before I leave today."

Holly stood. "Button or t-shirt today?"

Digger grinned and pulled to one side the lavender sweater she wore over a white blouse, revealing a button that said, "Family tree hugger."

Holly tossed a twelve-inch braid over one shoulder. "I like some of the others better."

Digger put the historical society issues out of her mind. The next few minutes passed quickly. Anytime she heard footsteps outside her cubicle, she knew it was someone who wanted to know what she'd heard about possible layoffs.

She hadn't been certain why she'd been called to the meeting with WMAA's charismatic owner, Dale Stufflebeam, and several staff from human resources. Toward the end, he asked for a list of all projects underway. Since Digger kept track, she finally understood why she was there and gave him the information. In essence, not quite as much in the pipeline as normal, but definitely enough work for current staff.

The request for a list of projects had reassured her. Surely Stufflebeam would be less concerned about work underway and planned if he intended to let some of the artists and marketing specialists head for the unemployment lines.

"Hey, Digger, baby." Holly's large brown eyes bore into her. "I'm back. I found Robert. He said you're sure our jobs are safe."

Damn Robert. "I told him I was pretty sure the meeting was a just-in-case type of thing. I'm not worried. I'm not a fortune teller, but I'm not worried."

Holly smiled. "I just enrolled in a softball league for this summer."

Digger smiled back. "Sounds like fun."

"Better be. Cost me forty-five dollars." Holly turned away.

Three-forty. Digger came in early so she could leave at three-fifty each day. She liked to walk a mile with her dog before dinner.

DIGGER PULLED HER CAR to an abrupt halt in her home's short driveway and slammed the car door. In her head, she heard Uncle Benjamin say, "Better a day late than a dollar short." He didn't mean it. He insisted on punctuality.

She raced up the front steps. She needed to be prompt when it came to Bitsy's late afternoon yard time, or her floors could be damp. Or the potted dahlia in the living room.

Bitsy barked. Urgently.

"I'm coming, Boy." But she dropped her keys on the door mat.

"Nuts." As Digger bent to pick them up, she thought she heard water dripping somewhere. *Weird.*

She opened the door, Bitsy bounded out, and water spilled over the threshold and onto her shoes. Only an inch or so deep, but no water should flow over her bungalow's hardwood floors.

"What the hell?" She turned and saw Bitsy next to the front yard fence, squatting and shaking hard.

"Come on Boy. We have to get inside."

Digger reached around the door jamb and pulled Bitsy's leash off a peg on the wall. "Come see me." She snapped her fingers at the dog.

Eyeing the leash, Bitsy approached, but slowly. Digger wanted to get in the house to turn off the water, but she couldn't leave her German shepherd outside alone. He could run into the street and get hit.

She ran down the steps. Bitsy backed up, then turned to gallop onto the sidewalk, making for the park.

"Bitsy! We need to get inside." She ran after him, but German Shepherds are fast. She grew close at the edge of the park, lunged through a mud puddle, and snapped the leash on his collar.

Bitsy sat, all seventy pounds of his frame balking against any command.

Digger glanced at her house, now a block away. "I know the water upset you. You can sit on the porch."

Bitsy let himself be led down the block. A laugh from another bungalow drew her attention.

"You get enough exercise, Digger?"

Mr. O'Bannon considered himself the authority on anything going on in the neighborhood. Thankfully, he didn't own a digital camera.

"Bitsy thinks he's on the 100-yard dash team." Digger didn't want to stop. She wanted to get home to check out the dripping water. "Gotta run Mr. O'Bannon."

"Tell the old goat I said hello." He waved her on.

No need to ask who he means. "Will do."

Digger urged Bitsy to keep going. Now that he was on his leash, he thought he could sniff every bush or fast-food wrapper. She almost pulled him up the porch steps and tied his leash loosely around a railing.

She turned toward her still-open front door. Water had stopped flowing out, but that seemed to be because the living room area rug retained a lot of it.

Where was the now very loud dripping coming from? Straight ahead of her, part of the kitchen ceiling creaked and fell. Too soggy to crash, the ceiling tiles turned into a pile of mush on the floor.

CHAPTER TWO

HOURS LATER, DIGGER stood near a living room window studying the estimate from her plumber. Even a month's pay wouldn't cover it.

Cameron Boyle, facemask pulled under his chin, shuffled his feet, waiting for her response. "I wish it wasn't so much, but those bathroom pipes are old. We'll need to replace all of them, including the ones leading up from the basement."

Digger glanced up at him. She'd known Cameron since high school. He wouldn't pad the bill. "I know. I'll have to find the money. Can I do it in maybe four payments?"

He frowned. "Since I know you, yeah, but the first one'll have to be bigger. I got a lot of pipe to buy, and I'll have to pay Jackrabbit to help me."

Digger smiled. "Better not let him hear you call him that."

Their classmate had earned his name because he sped around the high school track. And because of his humongous ears.

Cameron grinned momentarily, then grew somber. "Where will you and Bitsy stay?"

"Stay?"

"Well, yeah. It gets in the fifties and sixties in daytime but drops to the forties and upper thirties most nights."

"Fickle Western Maryland weather," Digger muttered. "I can clean up at work."

Cameron shook his head. "But you won't have heat or lights." He had turned off the electricity to avoid getting electrocuted.

"What? Why does it have to stay off?"

"A lot of wiring got wet, and it's old, too. Building inspector'll have to pass it. Probably some wiring'll have to be replaced."

Digger groaned. "Plumbing bills, electrical work…"

"And your ceiling." Cameron nodded toward the kitchen. "And you gotta get your floors cleaned up fast, so they don't warp."

She sat on the loveseat — the navy blue furniture had been delivered only two months ago -- and put her head into her hands. Bitsy, whom she'd put on a blanket on the loveseat, placed a front paw on her shoulder.

Cameron's voice sounded panicked. "I'm sorry, Digger. I shouldn't have talked about all of it."

She looked up. "Not your fault. I need to…"

Insistent knocking on the front door interrupted her.

Bitsy drew her paw back and barked.

A man's raised voice asked, "Beth! What gives? I see Cameron's truck here, and your porch is all wet."

Digger stood, every inch of her cold and stiff. "It's under control, Damion." She didn't move toward the door.

Cameron's expression hardened. "He calls you Beth? I thought you broke up with him."

"I did." Damion Horner was the last person she wanted to see. He had told her the three-bedroom house was a risky one to buy. He loved to remind her when he was right. Especially if it meant Digger was wrong. She didn't care what he thought. She loved her house, old pipes and wiring included.

"Beth. Open the door."

Through a front window, Digger could see the shadow of his six-foot frame on the front porch.

Cameron spoke in a lower tone. "You want me to tell him to go away?"

Digger shook her head. "I'll let him in for a minute. Could you stay?"

"Sure." Cameron planted himself in one of the hard chairs next to Digger's small dining table, just outside the kitchen.

Digger walked to the door and turned the lock. "Come in for a second, Damion."

She had no reason to be afraid of him. But he tried to badger her into getting back together every time he saw her by herself. In the grocery store, in the hallway at work, on the street. He knew her routine and Digger thought he watched for her in familiar places.

She opened the door and Damion strode in. He took in the living room with the kitchen behind it, and glanced to his right, toward the hallway that led to the two downstairs bedrooms.

"What happened?" He moved toward her as if to give her a hug.

Digger held up a hand, palm toward him.

Damion flushed, then smiled. "No germs."

*As if that were the rea*son. "Just a broken pipe. Cameron's going to get it all back together."

Cameron spoke up. "Lots of plumbing work. Probably be here a lot for a while."

Damion tightened his jaw but didn't acknowledge Cameron. He regarded her. "I can help you clean up, Beth." He started to take off his jacket.

There it was again. His refusal to call her the name she'd acquired — and kept — since age four.

"No thanks, Damion. Bitsy and I are leaving in a couple minutes to go to Uncle Benjamin's."

He frowned. "And leave this mess?"

"I've already called the insurance company. They're sending a cleaning team." She hadn't called yet, but knew her policy would at least pay to take away the destroyed ceiling and haul out and clean the wet rugs. She was pretty sure they would bring in dehumidifiers. *Damn. There's no electricity!*

"I'll help you carry that out." He gestured to her nearly new beige area rug. "It can't be saved."

"Probably can," Cameron said. "Most of the insurance companies send them over to Frostburg. Firm there dries 'em out and sanitizes them."

Damion shot him a look. "Well, aren't you just a font of knowledge there, Cameron."

Digger recognized Damion's condescending tone. He thought people who went to trade school instead of college weren't worth his time. Unless he needed his car fixed or something.

"Enough," she said, sharply. "I need to pack a couple things and get going."

She moved to the still-open front door and gestured toward the porch.

Damion hesitated and looked toward Cameron. "You leaving?"

Cameron smiled broadly. "Not just yet."

Damion's jaw tightened, loosening only enough to say, "Catch you later, Beth." He walked out.

Digger shut the door and leaned against it. "This day can't possibly get any worse."

Another piece of the kitchen ceiling came down, landing in the sink.

Cameron's voice shook with poorly disguised laughter. "Careful not to put that in the garbage disposal."

CHAPTER THREE

DIGGER SPENT THE NEXT hour-and-a-half on her cell phone talking to her insurance agent, locating candles and matches, and packing a suitcase. She decided to also take a hanging clothes bag and a couple boxes of stuff.

Without even a porch light, the dark house could look inviting to a prowling burglar. In the boxes she placed her laptop, small TV with its DVD player, and a bunch of odds and ends she didn't want to end up in a pawn shop with someone else holding the ticket.

She hung up after talking to her agent again and called Uncle Benjamin for the third time. Still no answer.

He'd be willing to let her and Bitsy stay with him for a week or so. She was the only one in the immediate family who liked to listen to his stories about their ancestors' journeys from Maryland to Kentucky to Missouri. Except for their branch, which stayed in Maryland. He'd have her as a captive audience until her electricity was back on.

But Digger hated to just show up. Lately Uncle Benjamin had hinted he might have a new woman in his life. Always on the lookout for those he called "foxy ladies," he'd had a dry spell for a couple of months. She didn't want to interrupt him if he and a new friend were lying about.

She finished a list of work colleagues to call tomorrow and then carried her boxes and suitcase to her Jeep Compass SUV. She came back in and hauled a large cooler from the hall closet and began to load it with food from the refrigerator. No sense letting it rot.

After putting the heavy cooler in her trunk, she trudged up the porch steps one more time. Bitsy had remained on the loveseat as she loaded the car. Digger regarded him. "It's too cold to stay here."

He huddled more firmly into the corner of the loveseat and pawed at his blanket.

"Come on. I put your food and treats in the car. You know you like to run around at Uncle Benjamin's."

Bitsy barked, jumped off the loveseat, and moved toward the front door. Then he turned around, padded to the stuffed chair in the far corner of the living room, and went behind it.

"Hey, I'm too frustrated to play…"

Bitsy emerged carrying his stuffed lamb and dropped it at her feet.

She bent to retrieve it. "Ugh." The back half was soaked, and Digger at first thought Bitsy had used it as a potty. Then she realized he had probably hidden it behind the chair after it got wet from being on the rug.

She scratched his head. "Smart boy."

Digger snapped Bitsy's leash on his collar and grabbed his blanket from the loveseat. After she put him in the SUV, she went back to be sure she locked the house. When they were settled in the car, his precious lamb on the passenger floor mat, she put in earbuds so she could call Uncle Benjamin again en route to his house. Still no response.

It was dinnertime in the mountainside town of 2,000 people, so Digger was able to drive without having to stop for anyone making a left turn from the narrow, uphill street. Half the time in winter and early spring the road was too slick to traverse easily.

People who lived on the winding route sometimes parked in the hardware store lot at the bottom of the street and trudged to their houses. Uncle Benjamin had owned the store for almost thirty years. He'd threatened to charge people for parking, but Franklin managed to convince him there'd be as much paperwork as if he were starting a new business.

Digger reached the top of Crooked Leg Road and continued toward Uncle Benjamin's. He'd purchased the house from his parents' estate and continued to let it be used for family gatherings. After her parents moved to the warmer climate of the Texas Gulf Coast, she'd spent most Christmases with Uncle Benjamin, much to her parents' chagrin. No way would she spend Christmas with palm trees.

She drove past the cemetery at the edge of town. She acquired her nickname there at age four when she accompanied Uncle Benjamin as he placed bouquets on family gravesites.

He let her wander — something her parents never did — figuring no one had ever risen from any local grave, so she'd be safe. From humans, anyway. As she wandered with her puppy Scamper, in the section called Baby Heaven, she'd followed him to a spot where the dog tugged at what looked like a half-buried stick.

When Scamper unearthed what she'd been sure was an infant's bone, she'd run screaming to Uncle Benjamin. He rescued what turned out to be a rabbit's leg from the possessive puppy, and her cousin Franklin had never let her live it down.

She smiled to herself. One of her earliest memories was his twelfth birthday party, when she was three. Born late in his parent's marriage, Franklin was closer to her age than her father's. First cousins once removed. When she followed him around his parents' house, he'd told her to go play with her toys. Eventually she grew up enough that he'd tolerated her, and now they were friends.

Outside of town, she squinted to be sure her headlights didn't pick up any foraging deer or a poacher who wanted to bag one out of season. Later in the spring, the drive would reveal dozens of pink or white dogwood trees, and in summer thousands of orange day lilies. Now, brown leaves still carpeted the land on either side of the road, but crocuses and a couple of brave daffodils poked through.

Bitsy barked at some perceived movement in the trees, but Digger didn't see a deer or raccoon. "Wishful thinking, boy."

The road grew steeper as she approached the family acreage. The current house, built in 1878, was the third on the property. The first had been a large cabin, and Benjamin's grandmother had the second one replaced with the current two-and-a-half story red brick structure. Digger had spent a lot of time on the wide, wrap-around porch as a child.

After he purchased the house from his mother's estate, Uncle Benjamin considered christening the place the Ancestral Citadel. Digger's father protested that it was no stronghold, and Uncle Benjamin said he regarded it as his sanctuary. It thus became the Ancestral Sanctuary. Digger loved the name and her uncle's tongue-in-cheek humor.

She passed the Gardiner home, which sat a quarter mile from Uncle Benjamin's. No lights on. They often ate supper at the Meadow Grove Café. Mrs. Gardiner hated to cook. Digger flipped on her blinker and turned right into the Ancestral Sanctuary's long drive.

She'd gone only a hundred yards toward the house when a car barreled past on the road she'd just left. As it sped by, its driver turned on the car's headlights.

Bitsy sat up, leaned on the back of the passenger seat, and barked.

"Who in the heck would drive up here with no lights?" *Damion.* "You're paranoid."

Saying it aloud didn't make her feel less so.

CHAPTER FOUR

AS SHE NEARED THE house, Digger felt comforted. Uncle Benjamin's ancient Ford F-150 sat in the small circle driveway. But no lights welcomed her. Not even the porchlight, which he usually turned on about four o'clock.

She grinned in spite of the darkness. "Bitsy, I think he may have a foxy lady in there." She stopped her Jeep Compass behind his truck and called his house phone again. He still didn't answer.

"I know he'd hear that, Boy. Maybe his foxy lady took him on a date, and they used her car."

Bitsy woofed approval.

Digger fastened the leash on his collar, and he whined. "There are no rabbits to chase this time of night." She didn't want him running into the woods after dark.

She tugged gently to get him out of the car. He barked once and leaned toward the front seat. "Okay, I'll get your lamb."

She picked the lamb off the floor and Bitsy took it in his mouth and got out of the car. Digger opened the SUV's back door to grab her suitcase. "Good thing he lets me keep a key."

Bitsy sat on the cold ground, so Digger reached again into the back seat and pulled out a box of dog treats. She shook it. Bitsy yelped, dropped his lamb, and stood.

"Pick up your lamb. When we get inside you can have one." She struggled up the porch steps, box of treats under the arm that held her suitcase, Bitsy's leash in the other. She let the leash drop as she reached for the door handle. Bitsy wouldn't leave his snack.

The knob turned. "Huh. He must have left when it was daylight." She let Bitsy precede her and flipped on the porch light and entry foyer overhead globe at the same time.

Uncle Benjamin's sweater vest lay a few feet in front of her, and Digger laughed. "I hope Ragdoll didn't pull any yarn when she dragged it out here."

Benjamin's huge cat often pulled slippers, socks, and lightweight clothes around the house when she was mad at him for leaving her alone.

Digger put down her suitcase and kicked the front door shut. "Ragdoll, where are you?"

Somewhere in the back of the house, maybe in the kitchen, the cat meowed, but it didn't come to greet them. Digger opened the box of dog biscuits and gave Bitsy one.

She sniffed. The house always had what she thought of as an Uncle Benjamin smell, a pleasant mix of old books, the pot roast he cooked in his crock pot every Sunday, and sometimes sawdust, if he had a carpentry project underway. Today there was a slightly sweet smell mixed with it.

"Uncle Benjamin? It's Digger and Bitsy." She hadn't expected a response. When he came home, hopefully tonight, he'd see her SUV.

Digger started to take off her coat but decided to bring in the rest of her stuff. When she had lugged the cooler into the hallway, she sat on it and pointed at Bitsy. "You aren't much help, Boy."

Bitsy wagged his tail and padded toward the kitchen, where Uncle Benjamin kept a bag of dog treats in the pantry. Digger stood, picked up the sweater vest, and hung it on the coat tree next to her jacket.

She glanced up the stairway on her left, listening carefully to be sure no squeaking bed indicated she'd interrupted a tryst. Hearing nothing, she passed the dark living room on her right and turned on wall switches as she walked through the dining room into the large farmhouse-style kitchen.

If Uncle Benjamin were here, he'd insist Digger turn off the foyer and dining room lights as she left those areas. She felt only slightly guilty about leaving them on. She wanted a lot of light in the dark house.

Bitsy sat on the floor in front of the pantry. "You just had a treat."

He pawed the door and Ragdoll meowed.

"Ragdoll, how did you pull the door shut?" Digger opened the pantry's pocket door and the cat sped out and ran up the nearby narrow stairwell that led to the back of the second floor. "Goofball."

Digger reached for the light chain and pulled. "What is that...?" But the source of the smell became obvious. Two glass jars had splattered on the floor. One held pickled beets, the other cinnamon apples Uncle Benjamin had canned last summer.

She turned and called up the steps. "You are going to be in so much trouble, dummy." Bitsy barked agreement and trotted up the stairs after Ragdoll.

Digger sighed and pulled the nearby trash can to the open pantry. Carefully she extracted the larger pieces of glass and tossed them into the can's paper sack. Uncle Benjamin refused to use plastic bags.

The apple jar had crashed more spectacularly than the beets. A good thing, since the beet juice would have splattered more. Digger decided to be thankful for small favors. When she was sure she had most of the glass, she took a dish towel from where it hung on the stove door and scooped up big chunks of fruit. She carried it to the sink and oozed the mess into the garbage disposal.

After she rinsed out the towel, she used it to mop the floor. She frowned. The sugar would attract the mice that found their way into the cellar for winter. Digger glanced at the shelf under the sink, hoping to find cleaning supplies. She didn't.

"Cellar," she muttered. It would be cold down there, but it would take only a second to get the pine-scented cleaning liquid and mop. Digger walked toward the steps that led upstairs, and opened the squeaky door to the cellar, which sat next to the back staircase that led to the second floor. The flap that let Ragdoll get to her cellar litterbox when the door was shut fluttered loosely.

Cool air hit her in the face. She flipped the light switch and ran down the steps.

"Oh, my God!"

At the bottom of the steps, Uncle Benjamin lay on the floor, knees pulled up to his chin, head tilted slightly up so his vacant eyes stared into hers.

Digger knelt next to him. She started to put two fingers on his neck, but drew her hand back. She told herself she had to do it. She extended her hand but closed her eyes just as her fingers got to Uncle Benjamin's neck.

No pulse beat there. She yanked her hand back and opened her eyes. Uncle Benjamin's skin did not feel as cold as she had expected. Had he fallen down the steps recently?

Digger stood. Tears coursed down her cheeks. "If I hadn't packed the cooler, I could have saved him." Her voice rose with every word until she wailed. "Why, why?"

Bitsy began to bark, his yelps growing louder with her cries. Above her, he raced across the hardwood floors, nails clicking. Digger could hear Ragdoll's high-pitched meows, the kind she made when another cat or a raccoon wandered into the yard.

Digger sank to the floor, and sat on her butt, legs crossed. She leaned forward from the waist and rested her head on her knees, sobbing.

Bitsy and Ragdoll ran down the stairs and slid to a stop on the cement floor. Digger sat up as Bitsy regained his balance. He dove into her lap and begin to lick her face.

Digger leaned back, half-sobbing, half-laughing. "Stop, Bitsy, stop!"

Ragdoll gently sniffed Uncle Benjamin's head and emitted a low growl. Bitsy walked off Digger's lap and put his nose on Uncle Benjamin's. That moved Uncle Benjamin onto his back, and she gasped. Slowly his knees seemed to relax and his legs straightened somewhat. He seemed more like someone sleeping.

She couldn't give in to her grief. She had to get the animals away from her uncle. He couldn't be licked back to health. "Come here you two. It'll be okay."

No it won't, not ever.

"We have to go upstairs and call...." *Who?* She clapped her hands. "Let's go."

Digger turned toward the steps, but the cat and dog didn't follow. Bitsy lay down next to Uncle Benjamin and put his head on his paws, and Ragdoll climbed onto Benjamin's chest and settled in.

Digger cried harder and fled up the steps.

CHAPTER FIVE

AFTER SHE CALLED THE sheriff, Digger couldn't make herself go back down to the cellar, so she sat on the top step. She hoped sitting there would encourage Bitsy and Ragdoll to come back upstairs. It didn't seem right to shut the door.

While she sat, she thought. Digger knew how to look up death certificates to find the cause of death of an ancestor, but nothing about how a doctor determined it. On their cemetery tromps, she and Uncle Benjamin discussed things such as how many local people had died in the flu outbreak of 1918. Never anything about when rigor mortis sets in.

How long had Uncle Benjamin been dead? Could Digger have saved him? If he had pulled his legs up toward his chin, he must have had time to realize he was chilled. Maybe he had been lying on the rough, cold cement for hours.

She placed her head on her knees again and hugged herself. *Stop asking questions you can't answer!*

The sound of gravel crunching meant a deputy had arrived. She stood and felt momentarily dizzy. She grasped the doorjamb for a second until she felt clear-headed, and then walked through the kitchen, dining room, and front hall to open the door.

Through the door's glass she could see Sheriff Montgomery himself ("of the first Maryland Montgomery settlers") on the porch. He knocked on the glass, squinted through it, and raised a palm when he saw Digger.

She felt her eyes tear again as she opened the door. "He's at the bottom of the cellar steps. I guess he fell."

Sheriff Montgomery pulled his mask up, frowned, and shook his head of thick hair. Digger could tell he was angry at the situation, not her.

"I'm sorry, Digger. You just found him?"

She nodded. "I unloaded my car, so I guess I was here about ten, maybe fifteen minutes before I called you."

Montgomery had been in the house many times, so he walked through to the kitchen. As he got to the top of the cellar stairs, Bitsy barked. "Whoa. What's down there?"

"My dog and his cat. I couldn't, couldn't make myself go back down there to get them."

Montgomery frowned. "Will they jump me?"

"Uh, no…"

"If you can't go down, call them up here." No please.

Digger drew an unsteady breath. "Bitsy, Ragdoll."

When neither responded, she grabbed the box of dog treats from the counter and shook it. "Better get out of the way, Sheriff."

Bitsy's bark became enthusiastic rather than wary, and he bounded up the steps. Montgomery stood aside and let the dog pass him. "What about the cat?"

Digger took a treat from the box and held it just above Bitsy. "Sit, Bitsy. I don't think she'll scratch you. She usually just runs away from people she doesn't know."

As Montgomery made his way into the cellar, Digger fed another treat to Bitsy. "I dropped your dog bed in the hallway. Go sit there."

Bitsy didn't move, just continued to sit and wag his tail. She gave him a third treat.

Montgomery's voice drifted up from the cellar. "Move, Cat!"

Ragdoll hissed and then meowed in a tone more akin to a shriek.

Digger closed her eyes briefly. From the sound of things below, Ragdoll would not relinquish her possession of Uncle Benjamin.

Digger decided on another form of bribery. She reached for Uncle Benjamin's electric can opener and pressed the top. Its whir brought Ragdoll up the steps at a run.

She walked to the cellar door and called down. "I'm shutting the door up here, okay?"

Montgomery sounded out of breath as he called up to her. "Fine, as long as I can get up there." With the extra thirty or forty pounds he carried, Montgomery appeared to huff as he squatted.

"You can." After she shut the door with her foot, Digger moved to the cabinet containing moist cat food. Ragdoll wound in and out of her legs as she grabbed the tab — no can opener needed — and dumped half of the smelly stuff into Ragdoll's bowl. The cat immediately began pulling the food into her mouth with her tongue.

Digger watched the multi-colored cat for a minute. Her moderately long hair hung straight except for around her neck. Only there did it stand straight out, almost two inches. The first time he saw her at the shelter, Uncle Benjamin had said she looked like a ragdoll, and the name had stuck.

Bitsy climbed off his dog bed and came to the kitchen door, tail wagging.

Digger pointed to his bowl, which had a few pieces of dry dog food in it. "You had three treats. Four if you count the one when we got here."

Bitsy whined, but Digger kept pointing. "You know you don't get that many." Tail no longer wagging, he turned and went back to his dog bed.

Digger sat at the small, red Formica-topped table in the kitchen. For the first time, she remembered Franklin. *Why didn't I think of him right away?* He needed to be told his dad was dead, but she figured she should wait until the sheriff came upstairs.

The adrenaline rush she'd gotten from finding Uncle Benjamin's body had worn off, leaving Digger spent. She folded her arms on the cold Formica and rested her head on them.

She stayed like that, motionless, for a couple of minutes. The only problem with resting was that her mind would not let go of the image of Uncle Benjamin on the cellar floor.

Then her internal movie channel brought up the broken jars on the pantry floor. Uncle Benjamin would never have left the pantry door open when he went down to get a mop or cleaning stuff. He'd know that Ragdoll would inspect the damage and could cut a paw.

Digger stood and walked the few steps to the pantry. Ragdoll couldn't get the pocket door open herself. Maybe the cheap ones at Digger's house, but not these heavy ones. And no way the cat could close herself in.

The sheriff's voice came up the steps. "Digger, I have a couple of initial questions."

Me, too. "Sure." She opened the cellar door a crack. "The animals aren't next to me."

Montgomery stood at the bottom of the stairs, one tan pants-leg now sporting a smear of concrete dust. "You can stay up there for now. Is he in the same position as when you found him?"

Digger shook her head. "He was on his right side. Bitsy put her nose on his and it made him kind of roll onto his back. And his legs stretched out a little."

He scowled. "Were the animals down here when you found him? I wish he hadn't been moved."

A couple of tears leaked from Digger's eyes. "When I found him, I started screaming and that brought Bitsy and Ragdoll down. They went over to him before I could stop them."

His frown eased. "I guess I can see how that could happen. But you didn't touch him, did you?"

More tears came, and Digger wiped her cheeks with the back of her hand.

"I am sorry about your Uncle Benjamin, Digger. I know you two were close."

"Yes." She straightened her shoulders. "I put two fingers on his neck, but I didn't feel a pulse. I thought…I thought he still felt kind of…normal, if you know what I mean."

Montgomery jotted a line in his small notebook. "I don't believe he was down here too long."

"Could I have saved him? If I'd come earlier?"

He shook his head. "I'm no doc, Digger, but he really banged his head hard. I doubt he was conscious for long, if at all."

His less gruff tone seemed designed to assuage Digger's potential guilt. She felt her shoulders relax. "Should I call Franklin?" She thought Montgomery's son had been in Franklin's high school class.

"I'll handle that. Write me a list of family I should call. Benjamin was your great-uncle?"

"Yes."

"Okay, I want to get this right. Your dad's Thomas and your mom is Shannon, correct?"

"Yes. If you have to call my parents before I do, please tell them I'm okay."

"Will do. I already called a couple of my people. I'll be up to talk to you more in a minute. I'll try not to keep you too long."

"Oh. My house…my pipes broke. I was going to stay here a few days."

"For sure not tonight. Investigators need to work. You have friends, right?"

Digger frowned. "Investigators?"

"I'll be up in a few minutes, Digger."

She shut the cellar door and turned to go back to the table. Bitsy and Ragdoll, sitting side-by-side for the first time ever, blocked the doorway that led to the dining room. Digger knelt on the floor and they walked to her.

Bitsy nudged Digger's head, so she sat on the floor to let the seventy-pound dog get on her lap. "Oof. You're getting too big for this." She reached out to stroke Ragdoll.

"I'm sorry you guys had to see that, especially you, Ragdoll." The cat sat next to Digger, out of reach of Bitsy's tail.

She took a deep breath as she comforted Bitsy and Ragdoll. It didn't seem likely anyone would push Uncle Benjamin down his own cellar steps, but how could they ever know? She wished he'd had some kind of security system, but he wouldn't hear of it.

After a few more seconds she gently pushed Bitsy off her lap. He trotted into the dining room, Ragdoll at his heels.

Her thoughts turned to where she would stay that night. Definitely not Damion's. Most of her high school friends had moved away, but she could call Holly from work. She sighed. She would have Bitsy and Ragdoll. Surely one of the hotels by Interstate 68 would allow pets.

Digger brightened. Her insurance company would probably reimburse her for a few days in a hotel.

Bitsy gave a muffled woof from near her feet. She looked down and smiled at the still-wet stuffed lamb he put at her feet. "Thank you for sharing." She picked it up by one leg and placed it against the wall, then washed dog slobber off her hand.

From the stairway came heavy footfalls as Sheriff Montgomery climbed up. Digger sensed his plodding steps also reflected sadness. He and Uncle Benjamin belonged to the same VFW Post. Uncle Benjamin was much older; he'd served during the early Vietnam era, though he didn't go there. The sheriff served in the second Iraq War. Digger remembered seeing them fold the flag together after a Veteran's Day event.

Montgomery shut the cellar door and looked at Bitsy and Ragdoll sitting with Digger on the floor. "You two rascals made my job harder. You contaminated a cri...death...scene."

Digger caught the word change, and her eyebrows went up." You think Uncle Benjamin was murdered?"

CHAPTER SIX

SHERIFF MONTGOMERY SPREAD HIS hands. "I have to investigate an unexpected death as if it *could* be a crime. I hope Benjamin will move to the accident category real soon."

Digger closed her eyes for a second. "Okay."

"You know of anybody mad at him?"

"He could be crotchety. I just heard some people at the historical society were still irritated about moving everything into those buildings on the square. But mad enough to kill him? No."

"Who told you that?"

"Oh." She didn't want to get Holly's grandmother in the sheriff's crosshairs. "Just someone at work."

"Digger."

She sighed and gave him Holly's name and office phone number. "But it's no big deal. I was at the holiday party after they got moved in. No one was mad."

Montgomery gave a brief smile. "Half of that group would fall over if they tried to take a swing at someone."

Digger didn't want to even consider that one of Uncle Benjamin's contemporaries had killed him. She tilted her head toward the kitchen table. "Phone numbers are there. Just Franklin and my parents. They should probably be the ones to tell my sister, Patricia. You likely know a lot of his casual friends."

Montgomery looked up from his notebook. "As I recall, he wasn't close to Clara's sister at all."

"I wish I could say I remember Aunt Clara better. I don't think I ever met her sister."

"Eunice." He grunted. "She never forgave Benjamin for wanting their boy to be named Franklin. I'll see if I can find her."

Digger hesitated. "I don't know how well they kept in touch. A couple times when I was with Uncle Benjamin and people asked about her, he'd say they hadn't spoken for a while." She paused. "And my father referred to her as 'a piece of work.'"

Montgomery grunted. "She had an opinion about anything. I heard she moved over to Morgantown. Somebody'll know."

Digger sighed. "I still can't believe he's dead."

Montgomery pointed toward the living room. "I need to ask you just a couple things. Be more comfortable in there."

As she walked in that direction, Bitsy and Ragdoll each stayed close, Bitsy as if he were tied to Digger's calf. Her glance swept the room. Uncle Benjamin often had a fire going on cool days, and the room felt abandoned without it.

Next to the fireplace was his large oak desk, and on a card table beside it two banker's boxes with his family and local history research. Digger could almost see him sitting at the desk, shoulders hunched over whatever he was reading. A bookcase to the left of the desk overflowed with material about Maryland history and a number of Western Maryland families.

Montgomery settled on the couch and Digger sat in a comfortable upholstered chair across from him. Bitsy lay on the floor at her feet and Ragdoll jumped onto a table in front of the picture window. As dark as it had gotten, Digger couldn't see anything in the yard. She supposed the cat could.

Bitsy yelped softly and she reached down to scratch his head.

"Nothing small about that dog. Why'd you name him Bitsy?"

Why is he talking about stuff that doesn't matter? "Because Mom and Dad gave him to me when he was really tiny. He slept in a square lunchbox I had used in elementary school."

"How long you had him?"

"Six years. He was a college graduation present. Dad wanted me to have a protector when I got my own place."

Digger stopped scratching his head, and Bitsy whimpered.

"Not all that brave now, is he?" Montgomery opened his notebook. "Did you talk to Benjamin at all today?"

"For a minute at three o'clock. From work."

"What did you talk about?"

Digger mentally went over the conversation. "I called to tell him I'd had some leave approved for a trip we were taking next weekend."

"He didn't mention whether anyone was with him?"

She shook her head slowly. He kind of teased me about some research, so in my head I pictured him sitting at his desk."

Montgomery jotted a note. "Not after three, then?"

"When I found out my electricity would be off, I tried a few times but he…"

"Starting when?"

"Maybe, oh, five-thirty. Five-fifteen." Digger took her cell phone from the pocket of her blue jeans. "Earlier. Five-oh-two. I got home from work about four and found the water leaking."

"You work at the advertising place, don't you?"

"Western Maryland Ad Agency. I work directly for some clients and market our company to potential customers."

"Were you a business major or were you into some kind of art?"

And you need to know this why? "I started college in economics, but I switched to history."

"Work on a lot of history out there at the ad agency?" Montgomery asked.

Digger sensed his sarcasm and didn't like it. "I help businesses here in Garrett County. And we do work for firms in other parts of the country. You just have to be smart."

Montgomery wrote again in his notebook. "Heard rumors about layoffs, since a lot of parts of the country were closed up for so long."

"We hardly had any COVID-19 cases here, so we didn't lose a ton of business. I hope not."

Montgomery went back to his notebook. "How many times all together did you…"

"I can look at the outgoing calls on my cell phone, but I also left a message every time."

"You know his password to get messages?"

Digger almost laughed. She pointed to Uncle Benjamin's phone, which sat on his desk. Next to it was his answering machine. "He's so cheap he still has one with a tape." She realized she'd just spoken of her uncle in present tense. She stood and crossed the room.

"Punch the play button with a pencil or something," Montgomery said.

Digger grabbed one from the desk and hit play. Nothing happened. "Funny, the power light is on." She peered into the machine. "What? The tape's gone!"

Montgomery spoke sharply. "Don't touch anything else on that contraption." He stood and crossed the room to stand next to her. "You're sure this is where the messages would be?"

Digger nodded. "The tapes are so old the outgoing message sounds kind of scratchy in a couple places." She turned to face him. "Somebody just took that tape."

"When was your last call?"

Digger crossed her arms and hugged herself. She barely whispered. "I called him from in front of the house. I had a hunch he was dating someone new, and I wanted to warn him I was here."

"Huh. Sounds like someone mighta been in here and heard you leave that message. You could've just missed them."

"But no one was parked out front. And why would they take the tape?"

The sheriff looked from her to the answering machine. "Yours might not have been the only messages on there." He stared at a spot above Digger's head for a moment. "No car in the drive. Speaks to some planning."

"I didn't hear a car start," she said.

He shrugged. "Plenty of spots where someone could pull over and walk in."

"Surely someone would have noticed," Digger began.

"How many cars were coming down the mountain the last mile or so when you were driving up?"

She frowned. "Not one."

Gravel crunched in front of the house, and it sounded like a heavy vehicle. As the sheriff walked to the door, Digger moved to the window overlooking the porch. The white van had the county insignia on the passenger door and the words "Medical Examiner" in big letters on the side panel.

Ragdoll jumped off the table and Digger snapped her fingers at Bitsy. He hadn't budged from his spot next to the chair she'd sat in. "Come on. We'll move your dog bed from the hallway to this room." Seeing her about to leave the room, he stretched and started to follow. But when she returned with his bed and placed it in front of the fireplace, he almost knocked her over trying to get in it.

"Good dog." Digger glanced at the clock. Eight PM. Since Uncle Benjamin's house was so far out of town, not too many cars would go by this late. That, and the fact that the house sat back from the road, meant that relatively few people would notice the ME van.

Thumping sounds on the steps made Digger look out the front window again. The sheriff had two people with him, an older man and a younger woman, both in trench coats over what looked to be white lab coats. Between them they hefted a gurney with a large black bag affixed to it.

Montgomery's voice carried to her. "I'll go down with you for a minute, then I'll be upstairs."

He opened the front door and led them in. "Digger, these people are Alex Cluster the chief medical examiner and his deputy, Penelope Parker. They'll bring in a couple more items and then work downstairs."

She nodded at the two masked people, and they both used the line TV shows employed, "Sorry for your loss."

Digger nodded again but didn't say anything. She went back into the living room and stared, unseeing, into the fireplace. She needed to tell the sheriff about the broken glass on the pantry floor. And she wanted to know when he would talk to Franklin and her parents.

If Uncle Benjamin had been killed, she needed to think more clearly. Who saw him last? And when? Had he really had a Foxy Lady in his life lately? If so, what did she know about Uncle Benjamin's activities today? And who the heck was she?

Behind Digger, Sheriff Montgomery cleared his throat.

She turned to face him. "I didn't tell you about the pantry."

At the same time, he said, "Are you sure you didn't see anyone heading toward town as you drove up here?"

Digger said, "Not once I got outside of town."

Montgomery asked, "What about the pantry?"

Digger pointed toward the kitchen. "I'll show you." They went to the kitchen and she opened the pantry's pocket doors. "The broken jars that were in here are what led me to the cellar." She relayed finding Ragdoll and the mess and seeking cleaning products.

Montgomery stared at her. "You mean you didn't go down there looking for him?"

Digger shook her head. "He hinted he met a new woman friend. I know it's not his regular genealogy meeting or anything, so I thought he was on a date. Or something."

"So it's just coincidence that you found him?"

"I guess you could say that. Because Ragdoll couldn't have gotten in the pantry alone, it probably would have occurred to me to check the house."

"We need to do that." Montgomery glanced around the kitchen. "Besides the pantry and answering machine tape, is anything off down here?"

Digger glanced around the room. "Not in here." She went into the dining room and slowly took in the heavy mahogany furniture she'd always been told Aunt Clara insisted they buy not long after they were married. The rest of the house had lighter colored wood furniture, usually oak. "Do you want me to open the china cabinet and buffet?"

Montgomery shook his head. "Later. Bathroom next."

That reminded Digger that she hadn't been able to use her own and she needed to go. "Okay, he generally used the one upstairs."

He nodded. "I know the one down here is an add-on. Believe he usually shuts it off in the winter so the pipes don't freeze."

To Digger's thinking, the main floor bath was in an odd location. Typical of old houses, there had originally been a bath only upstairs. A door off the living room looked as if it would be a small closet, but instead led to the half bath barely larger than a pantry. From the outside, it stuck out like a square boil.

She opened the door and they both stepped back.

Montgomery waved his hands in front of his face. "I don't believe Benjamin wore that kind of perfume."

Digger couldn't tell the brand, only that the overwhelming scent would sicken a dog. "I'll open the window."

"Hold on." Montgomery motioned that he would enter.

Since he would fill the space, Digger stayed in the living room. "I suppose this answers the question of whether he had a new lady friend."

"Or he mighta been trying to kill roaches."

Digger giggled for a second, then put her hand to her mouth, tears forming. "Nothing's funny."

Montgomery peered behind the toilet tank and on the floor under it. "Things will still be funny. It'll be hard to laugh for a few days." Seeing her fresh tears, he added, "You better be ready for a lot of good stories at his wake."

She nodded. "I suppose so. Did you get Franklin?"

"Nope. Left a message."

Digger's mouth dropped. "A message?"

Montgomery frowned at her. "Just asking him to call, not telling him why."

Cluster's voice carried from the cellar. "Sheriff. Come on down."

Montgomery raised his voice. "Be right there." He used his pencil to open the door of the medicine cabinet. "While I'm downstairs, take a look in here and see if the contents are how you remember them. But don't touch anything."

"Sure." Digger didn't need to be reminded that her uncle may have been murdered.

As the sheriff moved away, she stepped into the bathroom. The medicine cabinet was full. She remembered only a bottle of over-the-counter pain medicine (which varied depending on what brand was on sale) and some Band-Aids. Uncle Benjamin used to grumble that older skin was like paper.

Today, the cabinet held hand lotion, baby oil — no baby had been in the house for years, as far as Digger knew — and cotton balls. But the best clues to a female visitor were the mascara and false eyelashes. She studied a small tube and decided it must be eyelash glue.

The medicine cabinet door began to slowly swing shut, and Digger saw her reflection in its mirror. She expected her brown eyes to be puffy and red, but hadn't expected the streaked make-up and disarray of her shoulder-length brown hair. She could pass as someone who slept in her car last night. Or just lost someone they dearly loved.

She lifted her hair off her shoulders and let it drop again. Montgomery's voice startled her.

"Come out here, Digger. I don't want your hair on the floor in there."

She flushed. "Sorry." Digger moved back into the living room. "Definitely not his shade of mascara."

Montgomery chuckled. "Thought not." He grew serious again. "Anything else?"

"It's all different. Even the aspirin and Band-Aids are gone. They were the only things in there."

"And you don't know the name of the supposed friend?"

"No. Unless family's here, I don't recall ever seeing anyone else's stuff."

"So you think it could be someone really special?"

Digger shrugged. "Or really pushy."

CHAPTER SEVEN

THEY HAD TURNED TOWARD the living room when Digger's phone rang. "I can answer it, right?"

"If it's Franklin or your folks, please say hello and pass it to me."

She noted the use of please and glanced at caller ID. "I don't need to talk to Damion." She started to pocket her phone.

"Does he usually call now?" Montgomery asked.

"I usually don't answer his calls anymore."

"Why not?"

"Long story."

"Why don't you answer it just for now?"

Digger frowned, but swiped her phone and said hello.

"Beth? Just checking in on you." Damion spoke in his usual loud voice. Another way he tried to control a situation.

"No need to do that, Damion."

"Did you make it to your uncle's place okay?"

"Yes."

Her response had been clipped and Montgomery made a rolling gesture with his fist, which Digger took to mean keep talking.

Digger raised her eyebrows at him. "Did you think I forgot how to drive up the mountain to his place?"

"No. It just seems like a lot of activity up there tonight."

Digger straightened her shoulders. "Why do you say that?" She figured Montgomery could hear Damion's bellows, but she held the phone out to be sure.

"I heard the medical examiner is in front of your uncle's place."

Montgomery made a gimme gesture and she handed him her phone.

"Damion? Sheriff Montgomery here. Who told you that?"

"Oh, uh. Sheriff. Just, uh, in town."

Digger was pleased to hear Damion almost stammer his response.

"Where are you now, Horner?"

She noted his use of Damion's last name. Didn't sound too friendly.

"What's that, Sheriff?" Some static-type noise came over the line and then nothing.

"Hung up on me." Montgomery pulled a radio off his belt. "Car 4, you on your way up to Benjamin Browning's place?"

A man's voice said, "Yes sir."

"Stop the red Cadillac Escalade that I bet is about to pass you heading down."

"I see somebody driving kinda fast toward me. Ten Four."

Montgomery put the radio back on his belt and pointed toward the main stairway, off the foyer. "Let's talk as we head upstairs."

"Sure." Digger wanted to ask Montgomery what his deputy would do if he pulled over Damion, but she figured she'd find out soon enough.

She led the way. Behind her on the stairs, Montgomery said, "Not that I mind your business Digger, but I saw Benjamin at the VFW a few nights ago. He was real happy you weren't dating Damion Horner any longer. Why would he be up here?"

They had reached the 2nd floor, so Digger stopped in the hallway, which was lit with two night lights. She noted that each of the four bedroom doors was shut, which was unusual. The bathroom door was open.

She leaned against the wall, feeling drained, and faced Montgomery. "He says he wants to get back together, so sometimes he just shows up."

"As in follows you?"

Digger thought about the car that had rushed past Benjamin's driveway after she had turned in. "He knows my schedule somewhat. He also knows I'm not interested in getting back together."

"You worried about it?" Montgomery asked.

"I'm annoyed about it." She hesitated, then told him about the car that seemed to have been following her with its lights off.

"Huh." Montgomery loosened the collar of his tan uniform shirt. "Any reason to think he'd want to hurt your uncle?"

"He's a jerk, and I don't think he cares if we get back together. He's just so vain he thinks he should have been the one to break it off. But no, I don't think he would have hurt my uncle."

"Hmm. Light in this hall?" He handed Digger his pencil. She moved a few feet from him and pushed up the switch.

Montgomery looked around. "These doors usually shut?"

"No."

He pulled a pair of latex gloves from his right pants pocket. "You plan on touching anything, you ask me for a pair."

Montgomery's hands brought the word 'beefy' to mind, and Digger watched for several seconds as he struggled to put on the gloves. When he finished, he walked to the first door and opened it, touching as little of the knob as he could. He walked in first.

Digger knew this first guest room well. She slept here every Christmas Eve, and occasional other nights. The last time was in January, when they planned to leave at five AM for a drive to Washington, DC, to do some research in the National Archives.

She scanned the room. "I don't think anyone has slept in the bed since the last time I did. I'm the only one who puts the bedspread inside the spindles at the foot of the bed." Though probably a hundred years old, except for the mattress and springs, the maple wood on the double bed was pristine, and she thought the bed looked better with all of its wood showing.

Digger watched the sheriff take in the modern recliner in the corner and a side table by the bed. Then he glanced at the chest of drawers along the far wall, which matched the bed.

Montgomery crossed the room and opened the closet door. "Not too much in here."

Digger joined him at the narrow door. "The usual. Christmas decorations on the top shelf. Those are my clothes on a couple hangers, and my boots on the floor." She felt a pang of loss. She kept them here in case they wanted to head out to the family plot to put flowers on Aunt Clara's grave, or trim grass around the headstones. Last year Uncle Benjamin had Digger help him place large landscape stones around the edges of the cemetery.

Montgomery gestured that she should lead the way and they stepped back into the hall. Digger pointed. "The next room is another guest room. Then the door to the bath. The two rooms across from each other at the other end are Uncle Benjamin's and Franklin's."

"Franklin here much?"

Digger shrugged. "He has a busy job in DC, and it's three hours away. About every six weeks or so, and always at Christmas. At least once in summer he comes for a few days."

Montgomery opened the door to the other guest room.

Digger's eyes swept the room. "Looks the same." Her voice became unsteady. "He was going to replace that old recliner."

Montgomery crossed the room and opened the closet. "Nothing in here."

"Usually isn't. When my sister and her husband come, they sleep in here with their kids. They pack the closet."

In the bathroom, Digger saw only Uncle Benjamin's things. "Looks right. I guess his woman friend did her makeup and such downstairs."

As they stepped back into the hall, Montgomery's radio crackled. "Sheriff. Collins here. I stopped Mr. Horner. You want him up there?"

"Go over to him with the radio. I want to talk to him and don't want him hanging up on me."

After about ten seconds of silence, Collins came back on. "Here he is. Over."

"Mr. Horner," Montgomery said, "what are you doing up here tonight? And why did you lie to me about how you knew the ME's van was in front of the Browning place? Over."

"I knew Beth was heading that way. I wanted to see if she was okay."

Digger picked up on Damion's sullen tone.

Montgomery scowled. "She's been driving up here since she was fifteen. Why did you think she'd have a problem tonight? Over."

When there was no reply, Montgomery said, "Collins? Over."

"Sheriff, Mr. Horner is pondering his answer. Over."

"Deputy Collins, take detailed information on Mr. Horner's actions from about three PM until now, including anyone who can corroborate what he says. Montgomery out."

"Ten four," Collins said.

Montgomery put the radio back on his belt.

Digger stared at him. "Why three o'clock?"

"Your uncle probably died a couple hours after that, but because it's cool down there, it may have been as long ago as three PM. That's the ME's initial thought. Could change."

"I, you don't really think he did it, do you?"

Montgomery shrugged. "I don't think anyone did or didn't. I think the odds of you harming your uncle are 100 to 1, but I'll still need to ask you to account for your time. It's just a basic investigation technique."

"I was at work until just before four. You want to know more now?"

"Nah, not now. Come on. Let's look at the other two rooms."

"There's a third floor," Digger said, "but it's only partially finished."

"Swell." He opened the door to Franklin's room and he and Digger both stared. The clothes closet stood open with the wooden desk chair in front of it. On the bed were several medium-sized boxes. An open one showed baseball cards, and another the blue folders used for coin collections.

"Usually look like this?" Montgomery asked.

Digger shook her head. "Franklin wouldn't leave it like this. He hasn't been here for several weeks, as far as I know. And unless he asked Uncle Benjamin to look for something, he wouldn't have come in here and gone through Franklin's boxes."

"Let's look at…" Montgomery began.

A car came up the long driveway at high speed. Digger moved quickly to a window in Franklin's room, Montgomery behind her. A red Buick sedan almost drove onto the porch and a woman with long blonde hair ran up the steps.

Downstairs, Bitsy barked frantically.

"Ben? Benny? Where are you?" she called.

"You're faster, Digger, don't let her run through the house."

As Digger ran down the steps, she heard Montgomery behind her, cursing himself for not putting up the crime scene tape yet.

The front door was flung open, Ragdoll whipped around the doorway into the living room, and a wild-eyed woman about five feet eight inches rushed into the foyer. She and Digger almost collided at the base of the staircase. She looked behind Digger. "Where is he?"

Montgomery had finally made it to the foyer. "Ma'am. May I ask who...?"

"Where is my Benny? That van isn't for him, is it?"

When Digger continued to stare at her, Montgomery said, "Why don't you have a seat on this foyer bench for a minute?"

She tilted her head back and said, "No!"

Digger had a good view of her neck. Her face was relatively unlined, but a woman can't hide the age of her neck. Digger decided the blonde woman was in her early fifties, maybe older. And not a natural blonde.

Digger finally found her voice. "Who *are* you?"

"Ohmygod, you're Digger. Sugar, is he okay?"

Digger fought to keep her voice calm as Montgomery tried to steer the woman to the bench. "Please, I'd like to know who you are."

"Why, I'm Anna Jean Burke. Benny's fiancée."

CHAPTER EIGHT

DIGGER STOOD TOTALLY STILL. Montgomery placed his hand firmly on the woman's elbow and half-pushed her to sit. "Ma'am, I'm Sheriff Roger Montgomery. I don't believe we've met."

Anna Jean placed a well-manicured hand on Montgomery's arm, but looked at Digger. "Where is my Benny?"

Digger felt pretty sure that in all of his eighty plus years no one had called her uncle 'Benny.' "I'm sure the sheriff will let you know in a minute. I'd like to know how you recognized me."

Anna Jean blinked rapidly. "Well Sugar, the albums of course." She looked up at the sheriff, who had been studying her. "Please tell me where Benny is."

Montgomery cleared his throat. "I'm sorry to tell you that Mr. Browning appears to have fallen down some steps."

Anna Jean gasped and her eyes widened. "He isn't dead, is he?" She pronounced dead as a southerner might — day-ed.

"Yes Ma'am, I'm afraid he is."

Digger thought Anna Jean's reactions were exaggerated, but she tried to feel charitable as she sat beside the sobbing woman. However, when the supposed fiancée threw her arms around Digger's neck, she felt less sympathy.

Montgomery, still standing, tugged Anna Jean toward him. "Go ahead and stand up, Digger."

She did. Sometimes seeing a friend cry at a wedding or funeral would make her tear up. Not so now. "Ms. Burke, I don't believe I've heard Uncle Benjamin mention you."

Anna Jean looked up. "Why are all these boxes in the hall? Benny never leaves a mess."

"They're mine," Digger said.

Montgomery raised his voice slightly. "Ms. Burke, when is the last time you spoke to Mr. Browning?"

She sniffed loudly. "Early this afternoon. Just after lunch."

"So that would be when?" he asked.

About one o'clock. She smiled briefly. "He said he wanted me to come over to snuggle tonight."

Digger didn't know how to take this woman. Maybe she had been close to Uncle Benjamin. If that was the case, Digger didn't want to be rude. What reason would she have to feign closeness and grief? For now, she would accept that Anna Jean Burke and Uncle Benjamin had some sort of relationship, however recent. But fiancée? No way.

Montgomery had been watching Digger, so she gave him a slight nod. "Ms. Burke…"

"Anna Jean, please, Digger."

"Okay, Anna Jean. I'm sorry Uncle Benjamin didn't have a chance to introduce us."

Anna Jean took a tissue from a capacious red handbag. "He said he thought he'd do it this weekend." She blew her nose. "He said he didn't always introduce a lady friend, that's what he called me, to his family. He didn't want to rush into anything."

For the first time, Digger heard something that Uncle Benjamin might have said. "It would have been nice to meet you with him, instead of like this."

Anna Jean smiled brightly. "It sure would have been." She turned to Montgomery. "I'm sorry I kind of lost it there. Can you tell me what happened?"

He nodded. "I can tell you more in a day or so. Unfortunately, Digger found her uncle in the cellar. He appeared to have fallen."

She transferred wide blue eyes to Digger. "I'm so sorry you had to find him, Sugar." She took in Digger's suitcase and boxes. "Were you planning to stay overnight?"

Digger nodded. "My pipes leaked. The water's off at my place in town."

"Oh my, do you need a place to stay, Sugar? I know Benny would want me to help you out."

Before Digger could respond, Montgomery said, "She'll be able to stay in Mr. Browning's guest room this evening." He became very solicitous. "Now Ms. Burke, you've had a shock. Would you like one of my deputies to drive you somewhere? You must live nearby."

Anna Jean blinked rapidly. Digger didn't think she'd ever seen anyone truly bat their eyes. Maybe it was the false eyelashes.

"I live halfway to Frostburg." She took a deep breath. "No thank you, Sheriff." She turned to Digger. "Sugar, are you sure..."

"Really. I'll be fine here tonight. Maybe we can have coffee sometime."

"Well now, I'll see you at the funeral, at least." When Digger didn't reply, she said, "There will be a funeral, won't there? They're allowing them now."

"That's really up to his son, Franklin. Have you met him yet?" Digger asked.

Anna Jean frowned. "Benny was much closer to you, wasn't he?"

Digger kept her expression neutral. "They were close, too."

Sheriff Montgomery gestured to the door. "Let me walk you to your car, Ms. Burke. I'll get your phone number so I can update you tomorrow."

She picked up her handbag from where it sat on the bench next to her. "Why thank you, Sheriff. Uh, I did have a few things here."

"When we finish checking the house, I'll get back to you." Montgomery gave her a broad smile and ushered her out, offering words of sympathy as he did.

Digger shut the door and looked through the glass as he walked Anna Jean to her car. At the end of the driveway, she could see lights of a patrol car. *Too bad it wasn't there fifteen minutes ago.*

After a minute, the sheriff shut Anna Jean's car door and she started the engine. He turned and came up the steps at a brisk pace. He opened and shut the entry door quickly. "Cold out there."

"Do you know her at all?" Digger asked.

"No, and I'm sorry she..." his radio crackled.

A man's voice said, "Sheriff?"

"Montgomery here."

"Collins here. I was talking to Horner and she drove past. Sorry I didn't get to her before she got to the Browning place. Over."

"Doubt anyone else will drive up. Block the driveway until the ME leaves. Over."

Collins signed off. "Ten Four."

Montgomery glanced at Anna Jean's retreating headlights. "You never heard of her?"

"No. He asked if I was coming up here this weekend. Maybe he was going to introduce her."

Montgomery faced Digger. "She lives in Midlothian."

"She said halfway to Frostburg. That's just outside of it."

"Yes, it is. I'll make some inquiries. You hear more about her, let me know."

Digger nodded. "Sure."

Montgomery gestured toward the living room and Digger preceded him. "I said you couldn't stay here tonight, but I didn't want you with her until we know who she is."

They took their same seats in the living room, and Digger made an exaggerated shrug. "So I can stay here, or were you just putting her off?"

"That upstairs bathroom seemed almost sterile, and so did the guest room you use. After we finish upstairs, how about you take ol' Bitsy out to do his business and you settle in up there? Just use the bedroom and bathroom."

"I'm exhausted. And I need to do my business."

Bitsy came over and rested his head on Digger's knee. Ragdoll's head popped out from under the sofa, about a foot from Montgomery's leg.

"Hello, Cat." He stood.

"I wondered where you went." Digger bent to scratch the top of Ragdoll's head.

She found Bitsy's leash where she had left it in the foyer and walked him outside for less than five minutes. She wanted time to herself, and some sleep. "Come on, Boy. Do your thing." After Bitsy watered an apple tree for almost fifteen seconds, they headed in.

Ragdoll greeted them at the front door. "We won't leave you, girl." Digger unsnapped the leash and found Montgomery in the living room, staring at the papers on Uncle Benjamin's desk.

He turned to her. "Would you know if things are out of order here?"

Digger shrugged. "I'd probably only spot something really different. He mostly used that for family history stuff. He pays all his bills online."

"Okay then, head upstairs if you would. I'll come up in a couple minutes. I'd like you to look in a couple rooms with me."

"Sure." She picked up her suitcase from the hall and clicked her tongue in Bitsy's direction. When he realized Digger was heading upstairs, Bitsy ran up ahead of her, followed by Ragdoll. *What am I going to do with that cat?*

Digger put her suitcase in the guest room and used the bathroom. She noted her hair was still messy and decided it could stay that way until morning.

She had almost reached the guest room again when Montgomery called up to her. "Digger, make sure you stay up there."

"Sure." She heard people talking in the kitchen and heavy footfalls coming up the cellar steps.

They're bringing up Uncle Benjamin.

She hurried into the bedroom and shut its door.

CHAPTER NINE

DIGGER LAY FACE-DOWN on the bed and covered her head with the pillow. She didn't want to hear what the ME or anyone else said as they took Uncle Benjamin from the house. Muffled conversation floated upstairs so she pulled the pillow tighter.

After two or three minutes, she loosened the pillow and listened. Nothing. She swung her legs off the bed and sat up. Her feet touched Bitsy instead of the floor. His tail thumped and he opened sleepy eyes. When he saw no treat opportunity, he shut them again.

Where was Ragdoll? She heard a throaty meow from the foot of the bed. "It'll be okay girl. We can put a litter box in here tonight." *That should smell good.*

She stood, avoiding Bitsy's tail, and opened the door to the hallway. "Sheriff Montgomery?"

He crossed the kitchen floor and moved closer to the steps leading to the second floor. "Was wondering if you fell asleep, Digger."

She walked to the top of the steps. "No. Did you want to look around up here some more?"

"Couple minutes. I'm checking for prints near the coffee pot. Then I'll make some. Need some fuel."

Digger went back into the bedroom. She crossed to the window and stared out. From this room, she could see the large vegetable garden, now an empty plot covered in leaves, awaiting spring planting. *Which no one would do!*

Though she couldn't see it in the moonless night, beyond the garden was the family plot. A list in the family Bible indicated that nearly twenty people had been buried there, but only twelve grave markers remained. Not all of them were whole, or readable, now.

Uncle Benjamin said the earliest ones had been made of limestone from nearby, and had deteriorated over a couple hundred years. At this point, it was impossible to tell where the unmarked graves were, unless there was space next to a spouse and you knew their husband or wife was also in the plot.

A couple hundred years. She never forgot her family had been on this mountain a long time, but thinking about burying Uncle Benjamin in the small graveyard served as a strong reminder. He'd be next to Aunt Clara. She'd died about twenty years ago, and had been the last interment. Other relatives now preferred the city cemetery.

Sheriff Montgomery plodded up the stairs, so she went back into the hall. "After we look around, I'm going to grab a pan of clean litter for Ragdoll and get something from my cooler. I can eat some food up here."

He reached the top step, breathing hard. "Sure. Let's get back to Franklin's room."

Digger fell into step beside him. "Did you reach him?"

"Yes. He'll be here in the morning."

"Is he…how is he?"

"Shocked. Kept asking me if I was sure. He wanted to know about the cat. I told him about your pipes and said you'd watch the damn thing."

"I'll talk to him tomorrow. I guess it's his house now."

They stopped at the door to Franklin's room and Digger surveyed it again. "Did you tell him about the mess?"

"Plenty of time tomorrow. I don't want us poking around in here much. You see anything else obviously missing?"

Digger eyes traveled from the boxes on the bed to a large bulletin board over Franklin's high school desk. "I don't come in here much, but I think the board had more than those laminated newspaper articles about the track team." She frowned. "I think there was one Uncle Benjamin had laminated, about Franklin and his coin collection."

"I remember that. He won a ribbon at the state fair, didn't he?"

Digger snapped her fingers. "That's what it was. The state fair ribbon, too"

Sheriff Montgomery nodded. "I'll check with Franklin tomorrow. Can you handle going to Benjamin's room, or you want me to wait for Franklin?"

"I can do it." They walked across the hall and she held her breath as Montgomery opened the door.

The clothes thrown on the back of the easy chair in the corner were definitely unusual. Especially since a red sweater clearly belonged to a woman. "You know how Uncle Benjamin was about being prompt?"

Sheriff Montgomery kept staring around the room. "I do."

"One thing he always did was allow time to tidy the house before he left for anywhere. I didn't come into his bedroom all that much, but I doubt he left it like this on purpose."

Montgomery grunted. "Have a hunch who owns the sweater. Looking from this doorway, is anything obviously missing?"

Uncle Benjamin's antique oak furniture didn't match his hearty personality, but he said Aunt Clara picked it out, so he'd kept it. His bed with its modern-looking black headboard clashed, but it had shelves with lots of books about Maryland history. The tall chest of drawers stood across from the bed, and the bedside table had a pile of papers and a couple of books.

Digger took in the antique washstand that sat near the window. "Something used to be on that washstand." She paused. "Oh, an old-fashioned pitcher. I think it was from around the Civil War."

"Valuable, then."

"Probably a couple hundred dollars at least."

"Hardly worth the trouble," he muttered.

Digger thought of something. "He did keep a little cash in here, I think."

"You know how much?"

She shook her head slowly, then smiled. "Remember Y2K?"

"That thing where all the computers were supposed to go hooey when the year went from 1999 to 2000?"

"And half the technology in the country would have been a mess except a lot of geeks spent two years reprogramming computers to handle the double zero."

"What about it?" he asked.

"He joked once that he'd taken some cash out of the bank for Y2K and was still dipping into it."

"More than twenty years ago," Montgomery said. "Couldn't have been much left."

Digger raised an eyebrow at him.

Sheriff Montgomery scratched his head. "Benjamin was thrifty. I'll see if Franklin knows its whereabouts. Things like antiques, coins, they're kind of easy to identify in a pawn shop. Cash spends anywhere. Did he talk about it a lot?"

Digger shook her head. "But I remember a few times when he needed cash, like when Girl Scouts dropped off cookies one time, and he ran up here to get it."

"Hmph. Girl Scouts wouldn't come after him, but if he did it to an out-of-town delivery person, they might take note that he went somewhere in the house and got cash."

Digger suddenly didn't care one way or the other. "I'm going to get some cheese and fruit from the cooler and then get to sleep. Will you be here all night?"

"I'll have one of my deputies fill in for me sometime after midnight. You know most of them, I think."

"Doesn't matter."

"I trust my deputies, but I'd still say lock your door, case anyone else is around."

Digger studied Montgomery's back for a second. He'd known Uncle Benjamin for a long time, so she believed he would work hard to catch anyone who harmed him—whether intentionally or not. But she didn't remember a murder in Maple Grove or on the mountain in her lifetime. Did he know how to investigate one?

She couldn't really ask the question. As she began to shut her bedroom door, she realized she'd missed an important question of her own. If he was right and someone had been in the house when she called from the front driveway, where had they parked their car?

DIGGER WOKE WITH A START in the wee hours of Tuesday morning and groped for her cell phone on the table by the bed. Two-thirty AM. It took a second to remember she was at the Ancestral Sanctuary and not at home.

Bitsy stood from his spot on a blanket in the corner and shook himself. Ragdoll yawned from where she'd been sleeping on a towel not far from Bitsy. She stayed put.

Digger lay still, listening for whatever had awakened her. In the deep silence of a house in the woods, every sound at night carried. She thought she heard the kitchen door bang shut.

Bitsy came to the bed and put her nose on Digger's hand.

"You went just before bed. You don't need to go again." Bitsy tossed his head and went back to the corner.

Digger slipped out of bed and pulled on her socks. She needed to go to the bathroom, and wondered which deputy was downstairs.

Ragdoll slipped out of the room when Digger opened the door. She didn't want Bitsy to accompany her, so she shut the bedroom door, used the facilities, and stood at the top of the staircase. "Sheriff, you down there?"

She thought she heard a couple quick footsteps in the kitchen and the door to the back porch shut again. Maybe a deputy heading out for a smoke? But why not answer her?

Ragdoll padded down the steps and sat on the bottom one. She uttered a low growl.

"It's okay girl." Digger was halfway down the stairs before it occurred to her that maybe what she heard had not been a deputy. But that was silly. Sheriff Montgomery said he would leave someone. "Hello?"

No answer. Digger squared her shoulders. She had spooked herself. At the bottom of the stairs, a night light illuminated the front hall. The swinging door to the kitchen was closed, but a light shone from the crack under it. She cleared her throat so anyone in the kitchen would know she was coming.

"Sheriff? Deputy Collins?" When no one answered, Digger swung open the kitchen door. A can of Dr. Pepper sat on the counter next to an open toolbox. From the small whisk brush and tape next to it, she assumed the kit held fingerprint equipment. But where was the fingerprint person, or team?

Her eyes swept the room. Black smudges marked several areas near the pantry and steps leading downstairs. She touched the can of soda and found it ice-cold. Someone had just left, or was in the

48

basement. But no light shone under that closed door. And the back door stood open.

Digger opened a cupboard under the sink and took out a flashlight. She walked to the back door and latched the screen as she sent the flashlight beam across the porch and into the yard just beyond it. Strange. She left the screen latched but kept the main door open. The cool air felt good for the moment.

Only then did she realize her heart thudded in her chest. "Take it easy, woman." She walked toward the front of the house and peered out the front window. As she did, headlights turned into the driveway and started toward the house. The living room lights were out, and she stood behind the curtain until the markings of the sheriff's department became clear.

Digger opened the front door and turned on the porch light. She should have told the sheriff to leave it on.

She recognized Deputy Jim Sovern's rail-thin shape. Digger thought he usually worked in the office, and had heard he planned to retire soon.

Sovern got out and called to Digger. "Sorry to leave. The Gardiners next store thought they heard someone in their yard." He started up the steps. "Since I was here, dispatch asked me to check it out."

Digger opened the door to let him in. "Everything okay?"

He grinned. "I scared the crap out of an opossum and her babies under their back deck, but didn't see any extra humans around."

"Good to hear."

Sovern walked ahead of her into the kitchen. "Sorry I left the fingerprint stuff lying around. Did I wake you up when I left?"

Digger thought about that for a moment. "You probably left fifteen minutes ago, at least."

"More like thirty. I checked the area around their house pretty thoroughly." He picked up his Dr. Pepper and took a swig."

She stood in the kitchen doorway. "I thought I heard a noise about ten minutes ago. Did you, uh, leave the back door open?"

Sovern turned sharply and regarded the screen door. "I did not. In fact, I glanced to be sure it was shut. Didn't have a key, but I figured I'd be nearby. You think someone was in here?"

Digger shrugged. "I thought I heard some footsteps, but can't be sure. The open door I'm quite sure of."

He shone his light out the door. "Don't get many burglaries up here, but somebody could have been scared off at the Gardiners and come over here. Damn. I'll get some prints from the door, too."

Digger yawned. Since Sovern was back and the steps she heard seemed to have been headed out of the house, she didn't feel nervous, but she was exhausted. Would Uncle Benjamin's killer return?

Had Damion driven back up the mountain after the sheriff department finished with him? Not likely. He was arrogant, but not stupid.

Or perhaps a burglar who was thwarted at the Gardiners' house did try the unlocked porch door. The taillights of Anna Jean's car heading down the driveway came to mind. Did she know about Franklin's coins or Uncle Benjamin's possible stash of cash?

One thing seemed certain. Franklin really should put in cameras, at least on the front and back porches.

CHAPTER TEN

WHEN SHE WOKE AGAIN Tuesday morning, Digger couldn't remember why she was in Uncle Benjamin's guest room on such a bright morning. Then the image of his body sprawled on the cellar floor came unbidden and she sat up. "It really happened."

From her dog bed on the floor, Bitsy barked. Ragdoll roused from her place on the foot of the bed and stretched.

"Ragdoll, I made you a nice spot in the corner."

Assuming she'd been summoned, the cat did two quick hops across the bed and nudged Digger's hands for a scratch. Bitsy stood and shook her head, jingling the dog tags on her collar.

"Okay, we'll go out for a minute." Digger glanced at her watch. Six forty-five. Because of her late-night stroll through the house, she felt as if she'd barely slept.

She pulled on the jeans and sweatshirt she'd worn last night and unlocked the bedroom door. Both animals raced down the steps to the first floor.

From the top of the steps, Digger called, "Anybody down there?"

A man's voice carried up. "It's Charlie McBride, Digger. Jim left a couple hours ago. I made coffee."

She started down the steps. "Thanks, I'm going to let Bitsy out and I'll join you."

From the kitchen, Charlie said, "Hello cat. You want a treat?"

Before she threw the deadbolt, Digger clasped the leash on Bitsy. He gave a disgruntled yip.

"I'll let you wander later. I don't want to have to chase you now." Digger walked onto the porch and down the front steps. She crossed the driveway and stood on the grass to watch Bitsy smell around a small Christmas-tree sized pine that Uncle Benjamin decorated every December. Bitsy eventually found the perfect spot for his morning business.

Nothing made sense. Breaking into Uncle Benjamin's house would have been easy enough to do when he was out. Why enter when he was home? And the killer knew he was, because the truck sat in front of the house.

Uncle Benjamin never talked about having serious disagreements with anyone. True, he'd led the small group of historical society members when they proposed moving the society's collection out of the old railway station. Most people opposed the idea, but many came to agree with him after a summer storm tore off a lot of shingles and revealed rotting wood underneath.

He'd spent a lot of time last fall arranging for the move to the vacant building that used to house a print shop on the town square. By early December everything had been moved -- all the books, models of original cabins, Native American artifacts, and a copy of the map based on Deakins' original survey of the area. The map showed the 50-acre plots allotted to men who fought for Maryland in the Revolutionary War. All of the 2,400 plus Maryland land grants were in Garrett County.

Digger spent two weekends helping Uncle Benjamin and some of the more able-bodied historical society members get the new space ready for a holiday open house. That event had quelled most of the grousing about the historical society's move. Or so she thought.

Even though Uncle Benjamin had butted heads with people initially, in early spring Digger had helped him write a grant application to get funds to remodel the old railroad depot. Even the former grumblers had seemed happy it could be reborn as a tourist information center.

"Come on Bitsy. All those smells will be there later today." She trudged up the porch steps, still tired after getting almost seven hours of sleep.

Digger unfastened Bitsy's leash and headed for the kitchen. The coffee might make her feel more alert. She wanted to be able to help Franklin with whatever he might need today. She wondered if he'd told Sheriff Montgomery when he'd arrive.

Charlie stood when she entered the kitchen. A game of solitaire lay spread on the Formica-topped table and he looked as if he hadn't slept. "Sorry about Benjamin, Digger. He was a classy gent."

She grinned briefly and reached for the coffee pot and one of the mugs someone had placed next to it on the counter. "Not sure I've heard him referred to that way, but it fits. Thanks for hanging out here last night. When did you get here?"

Charlie ran his fingers through auburn curls. "I relieved Jim about three. Sheriff didn't really think anyone'd come back, but Jim said someone might have tried. Guess you can think about maybe putting in a security system if no one'll be here all the time."

"I take it Jim didn't find anything after I went to bed."

"Nope. Ground's dry, so it's not like a burglar would leave some size fourteen footprint in the mud."

Digger added sugar to her coffee and looked for the small cream pitcher that usually sat next to the pot. She didn't see it, so she took milk from the fridge. "I expect Franklin will want to do something. He should be up here this morning."

She studied the open refrigerator. "Are you the one who put the stuff from my cooler in here?"

"Yep. Once we finished checking for prints. I wiped down stuff after. Got rid of the black smudges."

"That was nice, thanks. You want some toast with cheese? I'm making some and there's plenty."

"Sure. We dusted all the rooms. I expect you can use the others upstairs after the sheriff goes through them with you and Franklin together."

Digger put bread in the toaster. "I didn't hear you upstairs."

"Sheriff told me and Jim to be sure not to wake you. Didn't do the third floor. It's mostly attic isn't it?"

"Yep. One area's been finished, but it's mostly storage. I haven't been up there in months."

Digger's cell phone rang and she pulled it from the pocket of her jeans. She nodded at Charlie. "It's Cameron. He's fixing the pipes in my house."

Charlie nodded as Digger answered. "Cameron. You're up early."

"Wanted to get a better idea of what I needed to order. Kind of dark in your house last night."

"I really appreciate that."

"I'm real sorry about your uncle. Wish I'd thought to drive up there with you last night, or something."

Digger put paper towels on the counter so she could butter toast and add the piece of cheese. "No way to know how I'd find him."

Cameron didn't say anything for a couple of beats. "Listen, I hate to tell you this, but I think someone deliberately put some small holes in pipes behind your upstairs sink. And behind the tub."

"You're kidding." Damion's face flashed through her mind. No one else would have messed with her plumbing. Or had the opportunity to.

"Nope. Thing is, I wasn't expecting that. I had my hands all over everything. I mean, if anyone wanted to check for prints, I probably messed up."

"I wouldn't give him the satisfaction of calling in the sheriff."

"So you think it was Damion?"

Charlie had gone back to his cup of coffee, but he looked up and pointed a finger at Digger.

"Who else? I'm in trouble, Cameron. Charlie's sitting here."

"You're still at Benjamin's place?"

"Yes, the sheriff let me stay in one of the guest rooms, and Charlie kept…everything safe."

Charlie gave a thumbs up.

Cameron chuckled. "And he has a mug of coffee right about now."

Digger didn't want to let Charlie in on Cameron's insight. "Indeed. So, do you need another check from me today, so you can get started?"

"Nah. I'll put it on my account at the hardware store. Your neighbor's letting me run an extension cord from their house so I have some light when I work."

"Mrs. Emerson? That's great." The toast popped up and Digger removed both pieces.

"Yep. And I've got plenty of orange cord. You want me to rent a generator?"

"If you need it. Oh, I need to call an electrician."

"Jackrabbit's brother's coming over in an hour."

That made Digger feel better. "Thanks. I forgot to do that. His name's Ed, right?"

"Yeah, Eddison Electric. Thinks it's a great name."

Digger grunted. "Okay. Franklin's coming up later. Unless I'm talking to him, I'll make sure I answer your calls."

She stuffed the phone in her pocket and pointed a finger back at Charlie. "He thinks someone may have put a couple small holes in my upstairs pipes. But he touched everything, so no prints."

"We should still…" Charlie began.

Digger shook her head firmly. "It was probably Damion. He was mad I broke up with him. But his prints are all over the house. It wouldn't prove anything if you found one on a pipe. He could say he looked under the sink to get toothpaste or something. And he'd like the attention."

Charlie scowled. "We'll see, Digger. I gotta talk to the sheriff about this."

There was no point in trying to out-stubborn him. She handed him a piece of toast and bit into the warm cheese on the other one. "Do what you have to do. I think I'll put some of my boxes back in my car. I don't want Franklin to think I assume I can stay here."

"You want any help?"

"No thanks. I bet the sheriff and some other folks will be here soon. Keep that coffee pot filled, will you, Charlie?"

He said nothing but took a bite and sat at the table again.

Digger unlocked the front door and stooped to pick up a box. As she turned, Franklin's black Volvo skidded a little on the gravel as he turned into the driveway. She pushed her boxes against the hallway wall and stacked the three of them.

As Franklin stopped his car in front of the porch steps, Digger called to Charlie. "It's Franklin, Charlie. I'll be on the porch for a minute." She didn't want him listening to their initial conversation.

Franklin jogged up the steps and enveloped Digger in a hug. "I'm so sorry you had to find him."

Digger had been telling herself she wouldn't cry when she saw her cousin, but her tears coursed onto his shoulder. "I should be comforting you."

Franklin, six inches taller than Digger's five-six, rested his chin on the top of her head. "Dad loved you like a daughter."

Digger pulled back and wiped tears from her cheeks. "Thanks." She fought her emotions. She didn't want to keep crying.

"Plus, you took care of his other daughter. That really helped me."

CHAPTER ELEVEN

FRANKLIN GAVE HER A firm pat on the shoulder. "Come on, let's go inside."

"Good idea." Digger turned to open the storm door, and as she did, Ragdoll and Bitsy squeezed out.

Franklin shook his head, but grinned slightly. "You guys are a greeting team now?"

"Ragdoll and Bitsy have been sticking together. Really funny to see."

Seeing that Franklin and Digger were headed inside, Ragdoll and Bitsy turned and pushed ahead of them. Once in the hallway, Franklin knelt to scratch Ragdoll's head, and he let Bitsy lick his cheek. "Whose patrol car is that?"

"Charlie McBride is in the kitchen."

Franklin stood. "Something going on out there?"

"I think Sheriff Montgomery wanted someone else in the house with me overnight."

Charlie opened the swinging door. "Hey Franklin, sorry about your dad."

"Thanks."

"Sheriff Montgomery's gonna stop by soon to talk more to you two. You wanna come into the kitchen? I can sit in the living room."

Franklin nodded. "I could do with coffee after my drive. We'll trade places with you."

Bitsy and Ragdoll stayed at Digger's heels as they moved to the kitchen. As soon as Franklin seated himself and placed his mug of coffee on the table, Ragdoll jumped into his lap.

Half an inch of his coffee slopped onto the table. "I don't think this cat's been on my lap in five years. Maybe more." He scratched

Ragdoll's head again, let her smell his hand, and gently placed her on the floor. "You'll be all right, girl."

"Your pants are covered in cat hair." Digger watched him brush off his blue dress slacks. She marveled that he'd had the presence of mind to wear a sports jacket and tie, albeit one loosely knotted.

Digger sat across from Franklin and he met her eyes. "You're pale and I've never seen you with circles under your eyes."

"I eventually did sleep. I guess you want to know…"

Franklin tapped the table with a finger. "Come on. Sun's out. I can drink my coffee while we walk to the end of the driveway and back. It'll perk you up."

They stood. Franklin called to Charlie. "We're heading out the back door for a short walk. Back in ten minutes or so."

The temperature had warmed to about fifty-five degrees and the bright sunlight made Digger squint. It felt good. "You left DC really early."

"Couldn't sleep much. I figured I'd drive up I-270 before the reverse rush hour."

Digger knew what he meant. A lot of traffic headed into the city, but it sometimes seemed as much headed up the technology corridor to Maryland's outer DC suburbs. Some people in Maple Grove took the Amtrak or drove to work outside DC. A few went all the way into town.

Franklin sipped his coffee as they walked from the back of the house to the front driveway. "The sheriff gave me basic information last night, and I don't want you to have to go over a lot."

"I probably don't know more than he told you. In fact, he's probably talked to Alex Cluster — the medical examiner -- and could know more about…how he died."

Franklin nodded. "Were you stopping by to check on Dad because you hadn't heard from him?"

"My pipes broke." Digger outlined her soggy kitchen and living room, and Cameron's thinking that someone may have poked small slits in her pipes.

"Good God. That's crazy. You can't go back there until it's safe for you."

"I think it'll be okay. More like I need electricity to live there."

"Are those your boxes in the front hall?"

"Yes, but I don't want to assume…"

Franklin interrupted her. "I can't be up here during the week at all. Not even every weekend. You'd be doing me a favor. Keep Ragdoll company."

They passed the cement hitching posts halfway down the driveway. Franklin nodded toward them. "Mom wanted Dad to take out those posts. She slid into one of them in a storm."

Uncle Benjamin had a faded photograph of a horse and buggy sitting in front of the posts, taken in the early 1900s. She hadn't seen it for a while. Digger smiled. "He said they were some of the oldest hitching posts on the mountain."

"All that history…" Franklin's voice trailed off.

"Was very real to him," Digger finished.

They had reached the end of the driveway and turned back toward the house when the sound of a car reached them. "Probably Sheriff Montgomery," Digger said.

His cruiser turned into the driveway. He stopped and rolled down his window. "Franklin, Digger. Wish it could be different for you."

"Thanks," Franklin said. "Just getting some fresh air. See you at the house in a minute."

"Okay." Montgomery rolled up his window and kept driving.

After few seconds of heading toward the house at a brisk pace, Digger said, "He was really nice yesterday."

"I don't know him well. You know his son, George?"

"Just who he is."

"He was in my high school class. Very embarrassed that his dad was the sheriff. Especially when the deputies did sobriety checks and arrested somebody's mother or father."

"George moved away years ago."

"Anything else you think I should know before I talk to the sheriff?" Franklin asked.

"Well, I'm not sure he'd like me mentioning this, but I don't want you to be surprised."

"I'm not sure anything about Dad would surprise me."

"Okay. Did, uh, you know he seemed to have a new girlfriend?"

Franklin grunted. "Don't you mean a new foxy lady?"

Digger grinned. "Can't believe I used another term." She sobered. "Her name is Anna Jean Burke. She stopped by yesterday evening and said she was his fiancée."

Franklin stopped. "No way. Dad and I didn't talk every week, but he'd tell me that right away. Besides, I heard him say fifty times he'd never marry again."

"Me, too. Maybe she was being hopeful." Digger waited to see if he said more.

""Kind of late for that. Did she know anything about his plans last night?"

"Just that they were supposed to spend the evening together." Digger decided not to say Uncle Benjamin had supposedly said he wanted to snuggle. "She was pretty upset."

Franklin resumed walking, and Digger fell into step. "Had you met her before?"

She shook her head. "Nope. She said he planned to introduce us this weekend. I wasn't sure whether to believe her or not."

Franklin glanced at Digger. "You didn't like her?"

"I didn't dislike her. She's kind of, I guess you'd say showy. Not his usual type. But what do I know?"

"More than I do," Franklin said. "I don't think I met the last couple."

"I didn't really meet any since that woman, Sarah I think her name was, a few years ago. Mostly I'd just run into him with a new person."

Franklin nodded. "I think he really liked Sarah."

"I think so, too. He told me just a few months ago that he wasn't going to 'integrate a new one into his life' unless he was sure they'd date for a while."

"Good old Dad, always the optimist."

They had reached the front porch. Bitsy's barking greeted them.

Sheriff Montgomery opened the front door. "Can I let this hound out?"

"Sure thing." Digger grinned at Franklin. "I think he's a little tired of the animals."

Bitsy bounded down the stairs, sniffed Franklin, ignored Digger, and headed for a large flowerbed to the left of the porch.

Digger noted yellow and purple crocuses had risen through last year's mulch and a few daffodils looked ready to burst into bloom.

They walked up the steps, and Sheriff Montgomery extended a hand to Franklin as they reached the door. "How about you and I talk in the kitchen for a few minutes, then Digger can join us again?"

"Sure," they both said.

Digger stood in the hall, near the entrance to the living room, and watched the two men walk into the kitchen. As Charlie greeted Franklin and offered him more coffee, she wandered aimlessly into the room and sat in a chair in front of the fireplace.

Everything felt so unreal. Surely Uncle Benjamin would call down from upstairs any minute. She stood and walked to the window. Bitsy sat at the bottom of the porch steps, apparently uncertain of whether to bark to come in or wait for her to come out.

Digger walked to the storm door and opened it. He ran up the steps, sniffed the floor for several seconds, and bounded into the living room.

"You must have had your Cheerios." Digger walked over to Uncle Benjamin's desk and studied the neat piles of folders. She knew his organizational structure. Piles for Maple Grove only, for Garrett County, and a final pile for personal family history materials.

The family history group looked like it had more folders than she remembered, but the top ones had been there for a while. She scanned the pile. Two new folders, neither labeled. She removed them and placed them on top of the others. She opened one and frowned.

Usually she and Uncle Benjamin talked about what he was researching, but nothing looked familiar. Uncle Benjamin had been a Browning, same as Digger. Aunt Clara's maiden name was Forsythe, and her family came to the U.S. much later than his. Uncle Benjamin had traced her lineage to the ship her great, great grandparents came on to the U.S. He'd had no luck learning more about her family in Ireland. This had frustrated him.

His ancestors had arrived in the mid-1700s. Relatively few people had come to the Western Maryland area at that time. Since there was no U.S. government to keep immigration records, he wasn't sure where the Brownings came ashore, as he put it. He thought Baltimore.

Fragile personal papers from the middle 1800s contained what an ancestor remembered hearing about life in the untamed wilderness of Western Maryland many years earlier. They described almost subsistence living, dependent on the animals they hunted.

Digger read the top page of notes in the first folder. It appeared Uncle Benjamin had been looking through old records he'd found and comparing them to some of the newer online information. She'd heard him grumble that just when he thought he knew everything, more state or local records had been digitized and loaded onto Ancestry.com.

Forsythe family names again. She smiled. Aunt Clara's birth certificate was on top. Clara Jane Forsythe, born 1943 in a hospital in Oakwood in Garrett County, 7 pounds, 3 ounces. Near the official seal was a tiny footprint. Mother's name: Mary Hanson. Father: Alexander Forsythe.

Digger realized she had not known Aunt Clara's parents' names. Most of the research she did with Uncle Benjamin was on the Browning side of the family, and he helped Digger trace her mom's family, the Muldoons.

Next was Clara's death certificate. Digger had never seen it. Only age 49. Cause of death was in a doctor's scribble, but seemed to match what she'd heard. Hemorrhagic stroke. Length of illness: one day. She died in the rural community hospital in town.

The next paper was a folded piece of expensive-looking, beige stationery. It had at one point been sealed with candle wax. Digger smiled. Probably from an historical society friend.

She unfolded the paper. In left-handed, flowery scroll, it read, "You should know that Clara Forsythe had a baby before she met you. She wanted to keep it, but her parents forbade it. I don't know who adopted the child, but you may want to find it. While there's still time."

Startled, Digger dropped the paper. She picked it up again. "That's impossible."

Or was it? Clara and Uncle Benjamin didn't even meet until she was out of high school, when he came back from serving in the military. Their gap in age wasn't large as older adults, but the eight years would have seemed a larger disparity until they were both in their twenties or thereabouts. Aunt Clara could have had a baby. But wouldn't she have told Uncle Benjamin?

CHAPTER TWELVE

FEELING LIGHT-HEADED, DIGGER shut the folder and placed it again in the middle of the stack. She leaned back in the chair and stared at the faded wallpaper in front of her. She drew a deep breath and straightened her shoulders. With almost shaking fingers she opened the folder again.

Underneath the handwritten note was a letter from an attorney. Digger didn't recognize the name but noted the attorney was from what she knew to be a larger law firm in Frostburg. She studied the letter without picking it up.

Dear Mr. Browning. I represent an adult in their early 60s, who is the child of your late wife Clara Forsythe Browning. I don't know if you are aware of the child, whom Ms. Forsythe placed for adoption at the age of two months.

I wish to assure you that this individual would simply like to meet you and learn more about their birth mother. The individual has had a good life, and makes no claim on any of your late wife's assets.

Please contact me at the phone number below, and I will act as an intermediary to set up a meeting.

Digger sat very still looking at the paper. The date on the letter was six months ago. She felt certain that Uncle Benjamin would have mentioned it, at least to Franklin, if he had met the person (man or woman?) discussed in the letter.

She also thought he would have told her about it. Not that he had to, but he might have wanted to talk to someone before or after he talked to Franklin.

She thought back six months. Uncle Benjamin hadn't taken any trips that she knew of, and she often knew his daily activities. She felt certain he had not met the now-adult child mentioned in the lawyer's letter.

She went to the page beneath the letter and found another one from the same attorney.

Dear Mr. Browning.

While my client is disappointed in your response, it is understandable.

They will not contact you directly. If you ever change your mind about a meeting, you may call or write to me at any time.

Digger glanced at the signature this time. The attorney was a man named Foster Davis. She didn't know the name, but why would she?

The page below the second letter from the lawyer was a pedigree chart for Aunt Clara. It noted her parents and three generations of ancestors, but the attached family history sheet indicated only Uncle Benjamin as a spouse and Franklin as a descendant.

It might be hard for Uncle Benjamin to think about Aunt Clara with someone before him, but why would he not agree to meet her child?

Voices came from the kitchen. Digger realized she had been reading the file for perhaps no more than three or four minutes. *How could the planet have turned upside down so quickly?*

She raised her voice in the direction of the kitchen. "I'm heading upstairs to take a shower and put on some clean clothes. I'll be quick."

Franklin called back. "Sounds like a good plan."

Digger stood still for several seconds, breathing slowly in and out. Then she headed upstairs. She would've liked to soak in the old claw tub, maybe get more of the stress out of her system. That would take too long, so she opted for a hurried shower and dried her hair quickly.

She kept seeing not the lawyer's letter, but the handwritten note. Who sent that?

Uncle Benjamin hadn't met Aunt Clara until the early 1960s. Franklin wasn't born until Aunt Clara was almost forty. Digger had once heard her mother call Franklin a miracle baby and assumed that Clara had thought she couldn't have children.

Did Franklin have a half-sibling somewhere? And what had Uncle Benjamin done when he saw that letter so many years after Aunt Clara died? Had she confided in him when alive?

Digger thought that the informal note, which in retrospect seemed almost like a threat, had come relatively recently. The paper did not appear old, and it had been near the top of Uncle Benjamin's file folders. Who sent it? The now-adult child?

Still preoccupied, Digger dressed in a pair of maroon, lightweight pants and a tan knit top and pulled her hair into a French braid. Then she remembered she hadn't called her office since she left her boss a voice mail last night. She took her cell phone off the dresser in the guest bedroom.

"Oops." She supposed she should have expected so many calls. She scrolled down the list. Three from Damion — "Screw him" — one from her office, and one from her neighbor. She didn't recognize a couple other numbers, but they were local. Probably from work friends she didn't have listed in her phone's contacts.

She called her office and waited to be put through to her boss, Abigail Davis. Digger didn't know who Aunt Clara's child was. Could it be Holly or Robert at work? No, Holly was way too young. Did Digger regularly see the person in the grocery store or post office?

Abigail came on the phone. She and Digger were the only two women in the admin suite besides support staff. Abigail, who was black, referred to them as the front parlor women. Digger didn't ask what she meant, but had presumed the implication was that they were two visible women — one a minority -- in a largely male organization.

Abigail's voice sounded truly concerned. "Digger, I got your message, and Damion filled me in on what happened. I'm so very sorry. I know you and your uncle were close."

Digger felt herself flush at the mention of Damion. "We were. And it was a big shock. My cousin's here now."

"I don't expect to see you again this week."

That was code for, "I really want to support you, but you know how I rely on you."

"Thanks. I'll check my email and let you know if there's anything you need to know. And, uh, do me a favor."

"Anything."

"Damion doesn't speak for me. At all."

After a couple seconds of silence, Abigail said, "I heard you broke up. He sort of made it sound as if you called him."

Digger snorted. "I did not. He's mad about the split and trying to get me to lean on him."

Abigail started to laugh, but stopped. "Sorry. None of it's funny."

Digger wanted to get off the phone. "So, you also got my message about the pipes. I'll probably stay with my cousin at Uncle Benjamin's place for a few days. You can call my cell if you can't find something about a project. I just started the drawings for the new quarry advertising piece, but it isn't due for almost two weeks."

"I'll try not to bother you. Let me know about a service, okay?"

Digger said she would and hung up. Abigail had given no hint that Uncle Benjamin's death was considered anything other than an accident. She was glad not to have to answer complicated questions. If Ragdoll hadn't been stuck in the pantry, she might not have any hint either.

Sheriff Montgomery's voice carried up the stairs. "Okay if we come up, Digger?"

Digger opened the bedroom door. "Sure thing." She hadn't made the bed earlier, and quickly pulled up the bedclothes and fluffed the pillows.

She needed to put the letters out of her mind for at least a few minutes, so she walked into the hallway. Bitsy greeted her, tail wagging. "Came up, did you?" She took a couple small twigs from his coat. "Were you playing with the wood in front of the fireplace?"

As the two men reached the upstairs landing, Digger could tell Franklin had been bothered by what the sheriff had told him.

Montgomery didn't give them a chance to speak. "I'm going to show Franklin his room and his dad's, if you want to join us."

"Sure." She blew Franklin a kiss, and he managed a tight smile.

They peered into his room, and the sheriff said, "You can walk in, Franklin. We dusted for prints last night."

"Did you put the boxes on the bed?" Franklin asked.

"No," Montgomery said.

Franklin shook his head. "Dad wouldn't have put them there. He wouldn't even have taken them out." He moved to the bed and glanced at the coins and stamps. Then he looked in the closet. "There was a small box, smaller than a shoebox, that had the best coins. Including a couple of silver dollars from the 1880s, a bunch of wheat pennies, and some silver dimes. You know, the ones they made during World War II."

"What you see is what was here yesterday," Montgomery said. "Why don't you look around more? Then we can check your dad's room."

Saying nothing, Franklin opened the largely empty dresser drawers, peered under the bed, and went back to the closet. After moving the remaining boxes on the shelf, he turned to them. "Not here. A burglar wouldn't have had to look too hard to figure the box had some value. I had it labeled something like, 'best stuff.'"

Montgomery grunted.

"But there's something more than the stamps and coins missing."

Digger thought for several seconds, but nothing came to mind.

"I had some early Pittsburgh Pirates' baseball cards."

"Barry Bonds, Senior?" Montgomery asked.

"Roberto Clemente's first year with the Pirates."

Digger almost stuttered, "The only year he wore number thirteen."

Franklin's eyebrows went up. "Didn't think you paid that much attention to the Pirates."

"You showed me that card like five times when I was about thirteen. I didn't know enough to be impressed back then."

"Probably why he showed you five times," Montgomery said.

Franklin's smile was grim. "I kept a bunch of Pirates cards in a box like a regular deck of cards. I always kept them in the back of the drawer of the bedstand."

Digger frowned. "Someone really searched this place."

"The playing card box was a good hiding place," Montgomery said. "But that other box probably looked like an invitation to the thief."

"I probably labeled it when I was twelve. Then I added more coins. Some of the more ordinary coins were in those blue cardboard folders you see in the other boxes. The ones in the small box were either loose or were in individual plastic cases. Small ones, for single coins."

"What's the Clemente card worth?" Digger asked.

Franklin shrugged. "Baseball cards are only worth what an individual buyer wants to pay, but I'd guess upwards of $1,500. Maybe more."

"Insured?" Montgomery asked.

Franklin closed his eyes for a second. "No."

Montgomery gestured and they followed him to Uncle Benjamin's room. "We didn't bother putting up yellow tape, since it would just be my people and you two. And like I said, we dusted already."

Uncle Benjamin's room had a lot of fingerprint dust smudges. To Digger's eyes, nothing had been moved when Charlie and Jimmy did their work last night.

"Notice anything missing?" Montgomery asked.

Franklin walked in the room and studied all areas. "There was a Colonial pitcher on the antique washstand."

Digger whistled slightly. "I thought it was from about Civil War time."

Franklin smiled slightly. "Dad would not be impressed, cuz."

"Worth a lot?" Montgomery asked.

"I don't know how much, but Dad had pictures of anything valuable in his safe deposit box. We can get one of his friends from an antique store to give us a rough estimate."

"Maybe your coins are in the safe deposit box."

Franklin shrugged. "I guess his attorney will know how to get into it, but I doubt it. He wouldn't have moved them without telling me."

Almost to himself, Montgomery said, "But why would a burglar want to kill him?"

Digger turned her head so fast her neck kind of popped. "For sure kill him?" She leaned against the doorjamb.

Franklin spoke sharply. "I thought you told her."

Montgomery ran his hands over his eyes. "I'm sorry, Digger. I had the ME's initial report just before I left my office."

Digger whispered. "How did he die?"

Franklin came to her and touched her elbow. "You want to sit on the bed?"

She shook her head slowly, looking at a photo of Uncle Benjamin and Aunt Clara that sat on the bedside table. Then she glanced at the sheriff and repeated her question.

"Cluster said his injuries weren't characteristic of someone who fell while going down the steps. More like if he'd been standing at the top and pushed, hard, and fell backwards." He paused. "Also some splinters in the palms of one hand, as if he tried to catch himself when falling backwards."

"But...couldn't he have slipped when he was coming back up? Like after he got some cleaning stuff?" Digger asked.

"There's a lot more to check," Montgomery said, "but there's another bump on his head the ME hasn't figured out yet. And no indication he got to the cleaning stuff. Course, maybe he wasn't headed that way."

"He would've been after he saw the mess," Digger said. "And he wouldn't have put Ragdoll in the pantry."

Franklin nodded. "Sheriff told me about that. He would have cleaned up the stuff on the floor before he went downstairs."

Digger smiled briefly. "I agree. Now what?"

Franklin took a deep breath. "I guess the sheriff will have some ideas." His phone buzzed and he pulled it from his pants pocket. "A few of my friends left messages on my cell phone. I need to make some quick calls."

"You two try to think more if he talked about anybody mad at him, anyone he expected to stop by…"

Digger shook her head, uncertain if she should mention the two-year old letters. But if Franklin didn't know about them, now would be a horrible time for him to find out.

Franklin looked up from scrolling through texts.

Sheriff Montgomery continued. "I have work to do, and you two need to plan a funeral, I'm sorry to say."

"We do," Franklin said. "Will you be here the rest of the day?"

"Don't see a need. We don't have a fancy crime scene crew, so I took some pictures yesterday, Charlie took more last night. That way we'll know how the house was arranged. You'll probably need to shuffle things around the next few days."

"Hard to think about all that," Franklin said.

Digger had some even harder things to consider. Why did Uncle Benjamin have the letters on the top of his folders? They had come months ago. Had someone contacted him recently? What should she tell Franklin?

Montgomery's cell phone rang and he held up a finger as he moved away to answer it.

Digger met Franklin's eyes. "I'll help you any way you want, but you don't have to, I mean, I'm not assuming…"

Franklin raised his arms in a partial shrug. "Who else would I ask?"

CHAPTER THIRTEEN

DIGGER WAITED ON THE front porch while Franklin answered some texts. She needed time to think. Staring down the driveway let her do that.

How did a child born more than sixty years ago even find Uncle Benjamin? Had his or her parents kept some adoption papers that named Clara? Perhaps the birth father, whoever that was, had been in the picture the entire time and finally provided the information.

Digger gave herself a mental head slap. DNA testing, probably. But wait. Uncle Benjamin wasn't related to the person. Franklin was, but had he sent his DNA kit back? Aunt Clara came from a very small family. What about her sister, Eunice? If the adopted child found Eunice, it wouldn't be hard to get to Uncle Benjamin.

Why would Uncle Benjamin not have wanted to know more about Clara's child? Was he concerned about not just that individual but others who could be brought into Franklin's life so suddenly?

Franklin's voice came from beside her. "Yoo hoo." He smiled.

Digger startled. "Sorry. Just…thinking."

He grew somber. "A lot to think about. Come on, I'll drive us downtown."

AS THEY DROVE THE FIRST quarter-mile, they saw three sheriff cars. "Another break-in, you think?" Digger asked.

"I bet they're asking if people saw anything late yesterday afternoon."

"Oh, right. I hope they find something." *Anything to catch his killer, whether it was an accident or not.*

Digger's cell phone rang as she and Franklin got closer to the funeral home. "Digger? It's Abigail. Have you got a minute?"

She mouthed the word 'work' to Franklin. "Sure. You need help finding something?"

"No, listen, I know this is not the best time, but we just heard at work. I think HR will call you."

"Heard what?"

"That stupid virus. In the last few weeks, we've lost 25 percent of our orders. They're laying off a bunch of us. Or maybe furloughing."

Digger didn't say anything for several seconds. She could see the pile of mushy ceiling tiles on her kitchen floor, and now no way to pay to get her house repaired.

"Digger?"

"Sorry, Abigail. I hadn't been expecting that."

"Expecting what?" Franklin asked.

"Layoff," she said, to Franklin.

"Nuts," he said.

Abigail spoke louder, and Digger held the phone away from her ear. "We get unemployment. It's not as much as our salaries, but it's something."

Franklin slowed for a curve. "Jeez."

"I appreciate you calling. I'd rather hear from you than on TV or something."

"Listen, you can…"

Digger interrupted her. "Franklin and I were on our way into town for some…plans. Can I call you back?"

"Good Lord, of course." Abigail sounded flustered. "Tell your cousin I said hello. No, tell him I send my best."

"Sure thing. Talk to you later." She hung up.

Franklin's smile was tight. "I heard her at the end. Guess I need to come up with a response when people say stuff like that."

"I think 'thank you' about covers it."

"I'm sorry about your job."

"I think it'll come back. And I'll get unemployment." Digger stared out the passenger window. She had only worked a few years at the firm. She bet she'd be lucky to get $200 per week. At the beginning of the pandemic the federal government had supplemented state unemployment income, but not now.

Franklin said nothing as they drove the rest of the way. Digger felt stunned. She knew less work was coming in, and half of her time was devoted to bringing in new business. They needed her. She had thought her job was safe, at most she might get her hours reduced.

Franklin turned into the funeral home parking lot. "You ever planned a funeral?"

Digger kept her face turned toward the window. "No. Did you help with your mom's?"

He turned off the car. "No. I was fifteen, and I didn't even realize that's where Dad had gone that afternoon. Aunt Eunice had arrived and he asked me to help her make sandwiches in case people came over."

"Would you have wanted to go with him?"

As they exited the car, Franklin studied the two-story Maryland Memorial Funeral Home, which had once been the summer residence of a coal-mining baron from Pennsylvania. "At the time, I wanted to be in on everything. As I got older, I appreciated not having to pick out her casket and clothes."

He leaned into the back seat to retrieve his sports coat and a manila folder. He stuck it in his mouth as he slipped on the coat. "They want me to prove Dad was born."

Digger preceded him into the funeral home lobby. She'd seen Uncle Benjamin's birth certificate several times. Born in 1935 "at home." She shuddered. And he would be buried there.

A tall man in a three-piece suit greeted them. "Franklin, Ms. Browning. Jeremy Hurst here. I'm so sorry for your loss."

Together they said, "Thank you," and Franklin smiled as he glanced at Digger.

"Just the two of you?" Hurst asked.

Good, he can count.

"Yes," Franklin said.

"Come into our family planning suite, and we can talk." He led them down the hall. To Franklin, he said, "Your parents must have had you later in their lives."

Digger thought it a rude point to make. What if Franklin had been adopted, or earlier children had died? *And what happened to Aunt Clara's much-older daughter?*

Franklin's expression stayed impassive. "I was a welcome surprise."

Hurst pulled on an elegant handle and gestured they should enter a large room. "It's always hard when you lose your last parent."

Could he be any more tactless?

Hurst followed them into a well-appointed room that contained two deep red loveseats and several upholstered chairs. In the middle sat a glass-covered mahogany table. A coffee service sat on a sideboard. Sprinkled throughout the space were small vases of silk flowers in muted colors.

Hurst pointed toward the coffee. "Would you like refreshments before we get started?"

Franklin's tone became businesslike. "I'm sure we'll feel free to help ourselves."

Hurst nodded and gestured to the table. "It might be easier to review paperwork at a table, but we can sit in more comfortable chairs if you like."

Digger and Franklin sat at the table, and he sat across from them. She felt self-conscious in her casual slacks and knit top, but she hadn't brought anything dressier to Uncle Benjamin's house the evening before. Franklin had simply knotted his tie and managed to look as if he'd just been with a tailor.

Hurst's information was uncomplicated. Uncle Benjamin had planned the service, drafted an obituary, and paid for everything in advance. Digger marveled at the simplicity of his wishes and smiled when she saw that he wanted the final song to be "When the Saints Come Marching In." He suggested that Franklin see if anyone from the high school would be willing to play the saxophone.

From a leather folder, Hurst removed a single piece of paper. "Your father did add this." He slid it across the table.

Franklin read it, smiled, and pushed it to Digger.

"I planned what I wanted, but you can do whatever you damn well please. Just don't spend a lot of money. Save it for yourself."

Digger grinned. "I can hear him say that."

"Me, too." Franklin regarded Mr. Hurst. "I do have one question. I don't know anything about family plots and how they are handled if a house is sold."

Digger tried to keep her face impassive. She had hoped Franklin would keep the house. But of course, it would be too much for him to manage from Washington, DC.

"There are state laws about access, but most sellers add a codicil at the time of deed transfer. Your attorney can advise you on specifics, but basically it says family members can have access to the plots." He paused. "I've known of a couple of instances where the sellers agreed to keep up the graves, and specified they would visit no more than a few times per year."

Franklin nodded. "I'll have to look into it all."

"About the obituary your father drafted," Hurst said. "You could read it here or take it home, but I'd need your input by this evening, if possible." He passed Franklin a one-page, typed document.

"It has to be this evening?" Franklin asked.

"The *Maple Grove News* only comes out weekly, and the deadline for this week is tomorrow morning."

Digger glanced at the obituary while Franklin talked to Hurst about timing for a service. Uncle Benjamin had few survivors, just Franklin and her own family. His two brothers and two sisters were named as predeceasing him. She thought someone who placed such stock in family history should have more. *Still time for Franklin to add to the mix.*

"Guys."

The two men looked at her.

"You might want to say he died in a fall."

Hurst sat up straighter. "Ms. Browning, it's not traditional to list the cause of death in the obituary."

"True," she said. "But if you don't, 100 years from now a family historian may assume he died of COVID-19. He wouldn't like that."

Franklin shook his head slightly but smiled. "We wouldn't want that, would we?" He addressed Hurst. "Add it. He did die in a fall; the issue is why he fell. We don't need to say it, the newspaper will cover the murder."

The semi-scandalized Hurst went over available times for a service. Franklin decided to have it at the funeral home on Saturday, followed by burial at the Ancestral Sanctuary. As they left the funeral home, Digger said, "It's not much comfort, but at least we can have a service now."

Franklin nodded. "The virus was never bad up here like down in D.C. I still wear a mask when I go to the grocery store. Almost anywhere inside."

"We were careful, especially your dad. But my office doesn't have a lot of people, and we have our own cubicles. We sprayed a lot of disinfectant and wore masks."

"Dad probably told you I worked at home for more than a month."

"He did." Digger sighed. "There will be a crowd at the funeral home, that's for sure."

"I'll call to be sure they have masks. Don't want all the town octogenarians to get sick at a funeral."

Digger smiled. "I can arrange for a meal at the house. I'm sure his friends will want to bring food."

Franklin nodded. "I don't like the thought of a dinner, but people will be hurt if I just shoo them off."

Digger opened the car door. "Maybe you can get Ragdoll to hiss at them."

As they drove up the mountain, Digger's phone rang and she glanced at caller ID. "Crud."

"What's up?"

"A guy I used to date. He pesters me to get back together."

"That Damion guy? Dad didn't like him."

Digger silenced the phone and put it back in her purse. "I liked his self-confidence, and at first he was very attentive. Later it seemed kind of...controlling. I think he even followed me up the mountain yesterday. Didn't turn into the driveway though."

"Jeez. Are you worried he'd hurt you, or try to break in?"

She thought for a couple of seconds. "No. It just ticks me off."

Franklin nodded. "Let me know if your big cousin needs to beat him up or anything."

Digger shook her head. "If I thought it would work, I'd get you to do it."

Franklin's phone rang and he took it out of his breast pocket. "Answer, would you?"

"Sure." Digger said hello and listened for a moment. "Okay, just a second." She covered the phone. "It's Samantha Silver, your dad's attorney. She wants to know if you would stop by so she can give you a copy of the will."

The winding road had no shoulder for Franklin to pull over, but he reached for his phone anyway. Digger handed it to him.

"Franklin Browning here. Does it have to be today?" He listened, frowned, and said, "Uh huh. Okay, we're only about halfway home. We'll come back."

He passed the phone to Digger. "She wants us both there."

"Gee." She thought for a second. "I don't need anything from Uncle Benjamin."

Franklin made a U-turn on the deserted road. "Not even all his family history files?"

"I bet those'll go to the historical society."

Franklin shrugged. "I like the idea of him leaving you enough to pay for your house repairs."

Digger looked at her watch. "I wouldn't argue with that. I need to let Bitsy out in about an hour. How long do you think this will take?"

"Don't know. We'll say we have to leave after forty-five minutes. It's not like she scheduled this in advance."

Samantha Silver's law office was in an unassuming brick building near the hardware store. Franklin parked and stared at the front door. "Dad said he was going to make some revisions to his will. Do you know what they were?"

Digger glanced at him. "We never talked about anything like that. I just hope he didn't put that Anna Jean woman in it."

"You think he liked her that much?"

She shrugged. "I never saw another woman's stuff at the house."

They said nothing as they walked into the law office, which Digger decided had definitely not been decorated to impress. The small reception desk looked as if it had been ordered online and assembled, and the furnishings in Silver's personal office weren't that much fancier.

Digger judged Samantha Silver to be close to forty, and knew the attorney had only moved to the town a few years ago.

She spoke quietly. "Franklin, we've not met, but I enjoyed talking to your father. He told me a lot of stories about Maple Grove during the post-World War II days." She nodded at Digger and shook hands with both of them.

Franklin smiled as he and Digger sat across from her. "He was about ten when it ended, I think. He always said the town was really alive after the War."

"It's definitely calmed down as mining died and tourists started traveling farther to ski." She pulled a folder toward her. "I don't have to file this immediately, but your dad's instructions were that I do so as soon as possible."

Franklin frowned slightly. "What was the rush?"

"I think to keep rumors from starting." She opened the folder.

"Why would that happen? Franklin asked.

Silver glanced from him to Digger, and back to Franklin. "Were you aware of the extent of your father's fortune?"

"Fortune? I never associated that word with him."

Silver smiled. "He was a saver, and he made some good investments in the late seventies and early eighties, when interest rates were high. He kept his money safe in a mix of mutual funds, and set up a trust to preserve the home."

Franklin's jaw tightened. "He doesn't want me to sell it?"

Silver's brows went up, but came down quickly. In a gentle tone, she said, "He doesn't want Ms. Browning to sell it."

For a few seconds, Digger felt very cold, and she couldn't have spoken if she wanted to. Franklin seemed equally mute.

Silver continued. "I think he was going to talk to both of you soon." She faced Digger. "Apparently you were planning a trip to the National Archives in a couple of weeks. Which is where Franklin lives."

Franklin stirred. "Not quite in the building, but not far from it."

Silver's smile was tight. "He said he was going to take the two of you to dinner at the Kennedy Center, and let you know his plans."

Digger finally felt able to speak. "The house is Franklin's."

Franklin stared straight ahead, seemingly at a wall clock behind Silver. "He probably guessed I would sell it."

Almost in a whisper, Digger said, "And that's your right."

Silver's tone became very businesslike. "Actually, it's not. Mr. Browning, Mr. Benjamin Browning, was very clear. The property goes to Di…Ms. Browning, with Franklin being permitted to remove all of his personal items and "other items that he and Digger agree on.""

Silver had read this from a handwritten note, which she placed on the edge of her desk, where Digger and Franklin could read it. "I said this informal note could lead to disagreements, but he seemed quite certain that the two of you would easily reach decisions."

Franklin half-turned in his chair and smiled, grimly, at Digger. "You can have Ragdoll and the litter box."

Digger shook her head. "You're assuming she wants to stay."

"She will." Franklin turned back to Silver. "If my father talked to you recently, was he sick?"

Silver shook her head. "I don't think so. He said the corona virus was a reminder that no one lives forever." She smiled and looked to Digger. "He said you and he knew which family members died in the 1918 pandemic, and he didn't plan to be a statistic in this one."

"Sounds like him," Franklin said. "What other surprises did Dad have for us?"

Digger wondered if somewhere there was a woman roughly twenty-five years older than Franklin who might show up and be an even bigger surprise.

"Were you aware that he owned two building on the square, the ones that now house the historical society?"

Silver seemed to interpret the shrugged shoulders and exchange of glances between Franklin and Digger as admission that they were unaware. "He said a few people, he didn't name anyone in particular, were angry that he had suggested the society move into that space. He bought them as he was arranging the move. It seemed to amuse him to know that he was bequeathing the buildings to the Maple Grove Historical Society."

Digger closed her eyes briefly. All the hurt feelings and annoyance could have been avoided if he'd simply said what he planned to do.

Franklin's tone was taut. "Any more major real estate revelations?"

Silver cleared her throat. "No. All other liquid assets, except for a modest trust for upkeep of the house and a few relatively small charitable donations, go to Franklin. At present asset values, Franklin will inherit approximately two-and-a-half million dollars."

That's what he was protecting Franklin from — a half-sibling who would want some of Franklin's inheritance. Shocked as she felt, Digger expected to see a look of surprise, maybe even pleasant surprise, on Franklin's face, not an increasing flush and a frown.

"I'm still paying off my student loans. Are you telling me he had that kind of money and I worked twenty-five hours a week while I went to Georgetown?"

Silver said, "I can only confirm the present value of the estate."

Digger said nothing, but felt tears begin to well. She loved the house, but Franklin had expected it. He might be angry at his father now, but his resentment toward her would build. Since she'd stopped pestering him as a pre-adolescent, they'd had a warm relationship. She didn't want to lose that. "Franklin, I…"

He continued to stare at Silver. "I'm not mad at you, Digger. I wonder if Dad had any surprises in his safe deposit box."

"I don't know. His instructions are that you remove the contents. He said your name was also on the box."

Franklin spoke stiffly. "It is. I'll open it in a day or so. Is there anything else we need to know now?"

Silver reached into her folder and pulled out a sealed envelope. "He left a letter for a Eunice Forsythe, whom I believe was your mother's sister."

Franklin stiffened slightly. "That's…odd. I didn't think they were in touch." He reached for it, and Silver put it back in the folder.

"What your father said was that I was to give it to her if she gave you any grief. I don't know the full context of the statement, but I gather she had asked for some of your mother's possessions in the past."

Franklin frowned. "Long past. I remember him packing up some dishes for her, things that belonged to my grandparents. I didn't pay a lot of attention to stuff like that."

Silver shrugged. "All he said was that he didn't want her to guilt you into giving her a lot of your mother's jewelry or other personal items."

Franklin turned to Digger. "Why do you suppose he cared?"

Digger smiled. "I think he always hoped there would be some little Franklins one day. Maybe he wanted you to pass things to your kids. She doesn't have any, does she?"

He shook his head. "Never married. That's not a prerequisite for kids now, but it was in their day."

Digger's stomach churned. She wanted to tell Franklin what she'd found. But she wanted a day or so to see if she could learn anything more before she handed him the information about a possible sibling. It might not even be true. There'd been no reference to a DNA test.

Silver glanced surreptitiously at a wall clock. "The estate is set up with me as executor, but there is no stipulation that the role can't transfer to you." When Franklin said nothing, she continued. "It's rather straightforward, so my work would not be terribly expensive, and could save you a lot of time."

Franklin nodded stiffly and stood. "I'd prefer you to handle it." He extended his hand across her desk, and she took it.

Digger stood more slowly. She also shook Silver's hand, then took a tissue from her pocket and blew her nose.

As they turned to leave, Franklin took in her reddened face. He smiled slightly. "The front porch needs painting. I'll help you pick a color, but you're doing the work."

CHAPTER FOURTEEN

IN THE LAW OFFICE parking lot, Franklin beeped open the car doors and Digger had her hand on the passenger side handle when a woman's voice called, "You-hoo. Digger. Is that Franklin?"

They both turned, and in a low voice, Digger said, "That's Anna Jean Burke." In contrast to her bright colors of yesterday evening, she wore a simple black dress with a crisp ivory jacket. Her gold necklace and matching large earrings had an expensive air.

Franklin turned toward her but did not move away from the car. Digger couldn't imagine the range of emotions he had to be feeling.

Anna Jean strode to him and grasped Franklin's hand. "Darlin', I'd been so looking forward to meeting you. I'm so sorry it has to be now."

Franklin accepted her hand-pumping for several seconds, and his stiffness made it clear he would refuse a hug. "Thanks. If I'd known of you, I would have called."

"My goodness." She glanced at Digger, who had walked around the car to stand near Franklin. "Didn't Digger tell you about me?"

"She did. Dad didn't." Franklin's tone was polite, but did not invite conversation.

"He was going to introduce me to Digger, and to you real soon." A tissue materialized and she dabbed at her eyes.

Franklin smiled slightly. "It's nice to meet you. If you'll excuse us, Digger and I have some plans to make."

Anna Jean's wide eyes turned to Digger. "I told you I'd help in any way I could..."

"You did. Thank you." Digger turned to go back to the passenger side of the car. "We do have to get going."

Anna Jean spoke rapidly. "I'm probably going to stay over here the next few days." Her tone grew almost frantic. "I hate to be pushy…"

Doesn't look that way.

…but have you made plans for a service yet?"

Franklin had already opened his car door. "We're just finalizing them. They'll be in the paper. Or you can look on Maryland Memorial Funeral Home's website."

They left an open-mouthed Anna Jean standing in the law office parking lot. Digger resisted the temptation to turn around to see if she had moved. "I can't help but wonder why she was looking for us outside Uncle Benjamin's lawyer's office."

"I don't wonder," Franklin said. "She seems to have thought he left her something and expected us to greet her like, I don't know, somebody special."

Digger waited for Franklin to say something else. After a minute, she said, "I'm sorry about the house."

Franklin expelled a breath and turned the car to go up the mountain. "I probably should have expected it. Dad loved spending time with you, telling you his stories, even cleaning up the family plot every spring."

"I don't know how all this works, but you don't need to move anything out." She flushed. Did she sound like someone who wanted to be in charge of the house?

Franklin took his hand off the steering wheel for a moment and waved it slightly. "We don't have to figure out anything now. Anyway, if Bitsy's soiled the carpet while we were gone, you get to clean it up."

Digger couldn't believe his almost cavalier attitude. She couldn't think of anything else to say.

Franklin turned onto Crooked Leg Road. "I'm trying to tell you not to worry, Digger. We just have to get through the next few days. Then we can talk more."

"Okay." Digger stared out the window.

"That Anna Jean woman said she'd be staying here for a few days. Where does she live?"

"Sheriff Montgomery thought she lived in Midlothian."

"Huh. I wonder how they met. Maybe she knew about his money," Franklin muttered.

As they got closer to Uncle Benjamin's, Digger spotted spurts of color near the road. "More crocuses. Uncle Benjamin and his neighbors planted a lot of them along the road a couple of years ago."

"Brighten the mood."

She didn't add that nothing would.

Franklin turned into the driveway. The sheriff's and Charlie's cars were gone, but Damion's Cadillac Escalade sat in front of the house.

"Crud," Digger said.

"That the ex?"

"Yes. I've told him a dozen times I don't want to see him."

Franklin used a John Wayne voice. "He's bigger than I am, but I could probably take him, partner."

Digger snorted. "I can handle him, but why don't you stay on the porch while I ask him to leave?"

Franklin pulled to a stop behind Damion's car. "Tell him, you mean."

"Yeah." She opened the passenger door. "Damion, why are you here?"

He stood from where he'd been sitting on the porch swing and made for the steps. "To support you, baby."

Digger noted his precise style of dress, which today included a three-piece black suit complete with a burgundy tie and a white pocket handkerchief. He dressed better than the funeral home director.

Franklin slammed his car door. "This is a private family time."

Damion stopped midway down the porch stairs. He flushed. "Digger and I are practically…"

"Not family," she said. "Damion, I've been really clear. You need to go."

He finished coming down the steps and stood a few feet from Digger. "Beth, you need me now."

Digger felt the heat rise in her face. "I don't. You need me to need you, and that won't happen."

Franklin now stood behind Digger. "Time to head back to town."

Damion's jaw tightened. He stared at Digger for several seconds, then turned abruptly and marched to his car. He jerked open the door and slid in. The car started with a roar and he pulled away from the house, tires spinning on the gravel.

After several seconds, Franklin said, "You'd better watch out for him. Guys like that don't want to be told no."

"And I have the leaking pipes to prove it."

DIGGER WAS ON HER OWN Wednesday morning. Franklin left early to drive to DC for a day of work. He planned to clean off his desk, as he put it, and return the next afternoon or evening.

The house seemed hollow without him. Digger and Uncle Benjamin had never lived under the same roof, but while she had been in the house a lot, she had rarely been in it without him.

She felt as if the notes in Uncle Benjamin's folder were calling to her, but she had a couple of things to do before she went back to them.

At Franklin's insistence, she was about to pound nails into the window frames so no one could raise the sash more than a few inches from the outside. Or inside, for that matter. She didn't expect whoever killed Uncle Benjamin to return, but Franklin didn't want them to trust fate. Digger planned to look at security devices on the Internet in the next day or two.

The house phone rang as she placed a bunch of nails on a kitchen towel, on the dining room table. She hadn't thought about how to answer the phone. "Browning residence."

Sheriff Montgomery said he had some information. "Is Franklin there, too?"

"He drove to DC to work for the day. Then he won't have to think about lawyer stuff for a few days."

"I have his cell. I'll call him in a minute, but I'll let you know now."

Digger's heart pounded. *More bad news?*

"I've been quietly checking on this Anna Jean Burke. She is who she says she is, far as I can tell."

"Did you really think she might not be?"

"Didn't have too many thoughts. She just kind of appeared in Maple Grove a couple months ago, met your uncle at the historical place, like she said."

"And she lives in Midlothian? There's not much there."

"Just off Interstate 68. Has a small house."

"That town makes Maple Grove look big."

"Yep. Grew up in Oakland and stayed until she was about thirty. Moved away for almost 20 years — got married and divorced during that time -- and came back to the area just a few years ago."

"What was her maiden name?"

"Hmm. Not sure I…here it is, Hawthorne. Does that name mean anything to you, Digger?"

"Not that I recall. She's not old enough to retire fully, is she? What kind of career did she have?"

Sheriff Montgomery chuckled. "She let people she met through Benjamin think she was in her mid-fifties, but her driver's license says sixty-three."

"So she still works?"

"I didn't push too hard when I talked to the minister in that little church in Midlothian. She hasn't committed a crime."

That we know of.

Montgomery continued. "I think she was more a bookkeeper than an accountant. Now she does some part-time work at Western Maryland Bank and Trust."

Digger started to ask a question, then decided not to. She wondered if Anna Jean had access to information about how much Uncle Benjamin was worth. Maybe she met him intentionally.

She tuned back into Montgomery as he finished a sentence. "…so, I'll keep my ears open, but she seems to be who she says she is."

"Okay, and you'll let Franklin know?"

"If I can't get him, I'll leave a message."

Digger went back to the hammering work. She lightly pounded a nail into a dining room window frame. From studying the city cemetery index many times she thought the name Hawthorne was there, but she only remembered it because of the 19th century author Nathaniel Hawthorne, author of *The Scarlet Letter*.

She flushed. In the 1800s, an unmarried, pregnant woman might have to wear a Scarlet A, but if Aunt Clara had a baby and gave it up for adoption, Digger couldn't imagine how hard that was. She felt proud of her.

She refocused. Today she would start to get the house ready to accommodate Uncle Benjamin's friends after the funeral. Her father had emailed her that they hoped to arrive Thursday afternoon. He was working on reservations. Digger would pick up her parents at the Morgantown, West Virginia, Airport. She hadn't seen them since Thanksgiving.

Her mom was big on 'chatting,' so after they arrived, Digger would only be able to do things that could be accomplished with someone sitting in a nearby chair. Mostly food prep chores, though she and Franklin weren't going to fix a lot of food.

The house phone rang, so she put the hammer on a side table and headed for the wall phone in the kitchen.

She was surprised to hear the voice of her neighbor, Mr. O'Bannon. "Now, Digger, you know I'm active in the historical society. A number of members are planning to come to the service at the funeral home and out to the Ancestral Sanctuary for the burial on Saturday."

"That's very kind."

"We don't want you to cook. We've divided up who's bringing what food. We need to send your uncle out in style."

She felt her throat start to tighten. "I'll have lots of baggies so you can take leftovers home."

He laughed. "You sound like that penny-pinching uncle of yours."

Digger knew he meant it good naturedly. "Do you know how many people are coming out? From your group, I mean?"

"We're getting up there, so there'll be more at the funeral home than at his place. Mrs. Jenkins said if she had to walk around the grave plots she'd fall and end up in one."

Digger envisioned the eighty-something society matriarch with her ramrod-straight spine. Mrs. Jenkins had been one of the most vocal opponents of moving the historical society to its new location. Uncle Benjamin bought her a corsage the day of the Christmas open house. She'd mellowed.

"It'll be good to see everyone. Oh. I just remembered. Uncle Benjamin wants someone to play *When the Saints Come Marching In* on a sax. At the end of the funeral. Do you know anyone, or should I call the high school?"

He grunted a laugh. "You know how it is in Maple Grove. Someone will know someone. I'll make calls. Do you need to talk to them beforehand?"

"I can't think why. If you find someone, I'll let Franklin know."

O'Bannon said nothing for several seconds. "Word around town is that you'll be, I guess, you are the new owner of the Ancestral Sanctuary."

Digger had spent time considering how to respond when people realized Uncle Benjamin had passed it to her rather than her cousin. "Yes. Franklin and I figure he thought I'd be less likely to sell it."

"Is Franklin…okay? I guess I haven't seen him in at least a couple of years."

"He's fine. We're both sad, and we were surprised at the will, but it must have made sense to Uncle Benjamin. Franklin said I have to do all the big chores."

O'Bannon's laugh seemed to carry relief. "Benjamin said Franklin's place in DC is historical, too. On something called Dupont Circle, I think."

"Yes. It's a three-story town home. From the late 1800s. He rents out the basement." She didn't add that he wouldn't have to do that anymore.

"Well, I won't keep you then." Contradicting himself, he added, "Looks like you're having a lot of work done at your own house."

"Trouble with some pipes. Have to replace them and the kitchen ceiling."

"Now that's a darn shame. You, uh, plan to sell it?"

"It's not something I can really deal with about now." Digger wasn't going to discuss her thinking with Mr. O'Bannon. It would be all over town. Plus, she wasn't sure what she thought.

When she could finally hang up the phone, Digger sat in a kitchen chair. She'd been trying to stay focused on getting the house ready for a crowd. It kept her from thinking about Uncle Benjamin's death. Murder.

She stared at the Depression Glass sugar bowl on the counter. Tomorrow men from the city cemetery were coming out to dig the grave. She could barely stand the thought of it.

CHAPTER FIFTEEN

DIGGER WALKED TO THE KITCHEN window and stared into the back yard, unseeing. After a few moments she gave herself a head shake. She needed to clean up the area around the plots. With winter gone, and even though spring started later in the mountains, there would be some flowers. And lots of branches to pick up, and probably matted grass to trim around the remaining graves. She wanted to do that during the afternoon sun. The radio said it would be close to sixty today.

Plus, she had to think about filing for unemployment. Uncle Benjamin said he'd left her some money for upkeep of this property. That wouldn't take care of living expenses and maybe getting her own house ready to sell.

She straightened her shoulders and went back to the dining room to finish putting nails in the window frames. An inelegant solution, one that Uncle Benjamin would not approve of. Later she could remove them and install something less hillbilly-ish.

Ragdoll lay in the middle of the dining room table. Bitsy sat on the floor looking from her to Digger and back to the cat.

"What do you think you're doing, dummy? You don't sit up there." She clapped her hands, but Ragdoll only yawned.

Digger stretched a hand toward the middle of the large table. Ragdoll leapt to the far end. Bitsy barked twice and thumped his tail.

"This is not a game." Digger moved toward the cat, which deftly walked to the other end of the table. "I'm going to get some water to spray on you." Not that Ragdoll knew what she had said. Digger hoped the stern tone would encourage the cat to vacate her spot.

After Digger circled the table a couple more times, Ragdoll leapt to the floor. Tail held high, she flounced into the living room. Bitsy trotted after her.

"That's all I need. Cat on the table when people bring food." Digger picked up the hammer and got back to work. The window that faced the back porch seemed the most logical one for someone to sneak into, since it couldn't be seen from the front of the house. She put two nails on each side of the frame.

She trekked upstairs to inspect the bedrooms. Franklin would sleep in his old one, and her parents would have the second guest room. Figuring it had been a while since the sheets had been washed, she decided to do that so the room would be fresh for them.

Digger had just finished stripping the bed when she realized she'd have to go to the cellar to do laundry. She hadn't been down there since she found Uncle Benjamin. "Damn."

She stuffed the sheets into the laundry chute in the hallway — originally a dumbwaiter — and got a clean set from the linen closet. She'd wash the sheets when Franklin was around.

After a second cup of coffee and half-an-hour of writing lists of stuff to do over the next two days, she headed for her room to change into clothes more appropriate for cleaning up the area around the plots.

From a cupboard on the back porch, she took a trowel, a small rake, and a pair of grass clippers. She also grabbed a brown paper sack so she could carry sticks and dried brush to Uncle Benjamin's burn barrel.

Bitsy was happy to accompany her and ran to the edge of the graves and back again, tongue hanging out, every inch of him happy. "Good dog. But we aren't playing with the sticks, we're picking them up."

The ground was uneven, but at least not mushy. After walking the 300 yards or so to the graves, she stood still to regard them. At one time there had been a fence around the tiny cemetery but it had deteriorated and Uncle Benjamin had removed it. The only remnant was a metal trellis with the word Browning in metal letters. About every five years Uncle Benjamin had painted it. It could stand a coat now.

Away from the protection of the house, the breeze had a cool edge to it. Digger counted the stones, as she had done many times. A number were simply unreadable pieces atop graves. Only twelve headstones remained standing and somewhat readable. A local stone mason kept them in reasonable repair. A battle that would be lost over time.

Only Aunt Clara's headstone would last many years. Her usually parsimonious uncle had commissioned a granite marker with raised lettering. Digger swallowed. It had Uncle Benjamin's name next to Aunt Clara's, but no dates.

A squirrel chattered from a nearby pine tree and Bitsy went to inspect the situation. "Don't wander, Boy." He wagged his tail but kept his eyes on the squirrel as it ran to a picnic table twenty yards away.

She first raked the area around Aunt Clara's stone, and was pleased to find a batch of daffodils had sprouted behind it. Purple tulips would pop up in a week or so.

Within half-an-hour, leaves and grass clippings had filled the tall bag. She was so engrossed in her work that a male voice caused her to yelp in surprise. She turned to face a tall man about her own age. She didn't recognize his blonde hair or awkward stance, and her heart pounded.

"I'm sorry. I knocked at the front door." He almost stammered, "You're Benjamin Browning's niece, aren't you? Do you have a minute?"

His discomfort calmed her. As she studied him further, she realized the small spiral notebook and pencil stuck in it were the tools of a reporter.

"Yes. Beth Browning, but everyone calls me Digger."

The man glanced at the trowel in her hand, and grinned. "Guess I know why. I'm Marty Hofstedder from the *Maple Grove News*."

"Right. I think the funeral home was going to send you his obituary." Why else would the man drive all the way out here? *Because he heard Uncle Benjamin was murdered.*

"I am sorry about Mr. Browning. I interviewed him about a year ago, when he kind of led the charge to move the historical society out of the old train depot."

"His claim to fame." Digger didn't offer more.

Hofstedder pushed horn-rimmed glasses more firmly onto his nose. "I know it's not easy to talk about, but I read the medical examiner's initial report. It sounds as if your uncle didn't die from a fall."

"I've heard that."

"You aren't going to make this easy, are you?"

Digger tossed the wad of dry grass she'd been holding into the bag. "You haven't asked me a question yet."

Hofstedder grinned, a lopsided action that showed very straight teeth. "True." The grin faded. "I believe you found him. Do you think your uncle was murdered?"

She shrugged. "He was on the floor in the cellar. It didn't occur to me that it was anything but a fall. He had already…died."

Bitsy began to bark, the sound growing closer. Digger called to him. "Some guard dog."

Bitsy barked until she stood next to Digger. "Hush. He's okay."

Hofstedder reached into the pocket of his pants and pulled out a plastic baggie with a dog treat. "I never know what I'll find, so I carry these…"

Bitsy already had her nose at his hand. Digger smiled. "You can give it to him."

Hofstedder unwrapped it and opened his hand for Bitsy to take it. Dog slobber remained. He shook his hand. "Occupational hazard."

Digger pulled a tissue from a pocket. "I've been keeping these close."

He took it, wiped his hand, and tossed it in the sack of branches. "Thanks." He flipped a page in his notebook. "The ME seemed to think one head trauma was from something other than the fall."

Digger had felt a brief sense of connection with the man, but now kept her face impassive. "Really, you'll have to get your information from the ME or the sheriff." She gestured to the plots around her. "My focus is on getting ready for the funeral and after."

Hofstedder's eyebrows went up, which caused his glasses to slide down his nose again. "He's being buried here? I thought, I assumed you were doing spring clean-up."

Digger gave him a cold stare.

He flushed. "I mean, we do that at the plots behind my grandparents' house. But their little cemetery isn't used anymore. Added to, or whatever you say."

Digger found his discomfort humanizing. "Who are your grandparents?"

"Maria and Malcolm Wilson."

Digger smiled. "Uncle Benjamin called them the Double M's."

His flush lessened and the glasses went back up the nose. "A bunch of their friends call them that. I wasn't sure how well they knew your uncle."

"I'm not sure either, but I've been with him when he ran into them, like in the coffee shop. They always talked for a minute." She wondered why she hadn't seen Marty Hofstedder around town.

"I only moved here a couple of years ago. I grew up closer to the Eastern Shore and had a job with the *Baltimore Sun* but, you know, layoffs. I came to visit for a couple of weeks and stayed."

"This place grows on you." Digger waited for him to ask a question. She had no idea what Franklin would think about a reporter digging into his father's death. No way would she prolong the conversation.

Hofstedder cleared his throat. "So, can you think of anyone who would want to hurt your uncle?"

"Two points. You need to direct any questions like that to the sheriff. Second, no, of course not. But I'm not going to talk about any of it. With anybody." She especially wasn't going to give him her opinion on broken jars of canned food and Ragdoll being stuck in the pantry.

He nodded. "Sure. Is your cousin around? Franklin?"

Digger shook her head. "He went back to DC to handle some work stuff. He'll be back tomorrow. He wanted to finish some work so he could stay here for a few days without thinking about it." She didn't offer Franklin's phone number.

Hofstedder seemed to sense Digger would be true to her word and not comment more. He shut his notebook. "Just one more thing. What do you most remember about your uncle, or would you want other people to remember?"

Digger hesitated. "You know what a history buff he was. He thought our futures would be better if we knew more about our past. You know the quote."

"Churchill's speech to Parliament. 'Those who fail to learn from history are condemned to repeat it.'"

"Actually," Digger smiled, "Churchill adapted it from a George Santayana quote from earlier in the 20th century."

Eyebrows up again, glasses down the nose. "Aren't you the history buff."

"Kind of." She retrieved her trowel from next to the bag of yard waste.

"Okay then, thanks for talking to me."

"Sure." As he began to walk away, Digger bent to uproot a huge weed.

Bitsy trotted after Hofstedder. He stopped and turned toward her again. "One more thing. It's such a great old house. Do you think your cousin will sell it?"

Digger didn't want the paper to mention she now owned the Ancestral Sanctuary. "I'm pretty sure it will stay in the family. At least for a time."

He grinned. "My grandparents hoped you'd say that." He turned and continued toward the front of the house. Over his shoulder, he called, "Nice shirt."

Digger glanced down. She'd forgotten she was wearing a long-sleeved cotton shirt that said, "I dig dead people."

She called for Bitsy, who reluctantly came toward her, and watched Hofstedder's retreating back for several seconds. Then she studied the grave markers again. There wasn't much more she could do without committing to an afternoon with a stiff rake. She didn't want the sore back that would provide, or the need for a shower. She planned to head down to the historical society to see if there was more to be learned about Aunt Clara and a baby from roughly sixty years ago.

CHAPTER SIXTEEN

DIGGER CALLED AHEAD TO see if anyone would be at the Maple Grove Historical Society. She told the very sad Mrs. Zorn that she wanted to look at some of the articles Uncle Benjamin had written, and maybe take digital shots of any old photos of him. "I want to put some things on a bulletin board we'll take to the funeral home."

"Doug O'Bannon and I were just talking about pictures of him. I've got some ideas of where to look."

Digger groaned inwardly. She didn't want Mrs. Zorn at her elbow. She'd have to let her help for a time, and then she'd say she wanted to wander the two rooms. Digger had helped Uncle Benjamin and a few other dedicated souls set up the displays after the move. She'd say she wanted to treasure the memories in private.

She didn't want to take a physical copy of the note or letters from the lawyer, so she snapped pictures with her phone.

She checked the downstairs bathroom mirror — the room no longer smelling like a flower shop or den of iniquity — and applied lipstick. She decided to change tops because hers had pieces of sticks and leaves in it. She dashed upstairs, and within three minutes was back down and locking the front door on her way out.

As she drove down the mountain, Digger kept seeing the image of the handwritten note. There was no way to tell if Clara really had a baby before she met Uncle Benjamin. And she had a sister. Why send the note to Benjamin when a sister might have more knowledge of a child?

Had the pregnancy been the result of a crime? Surely not. Or maybe it was all fake. A nasty joke, or an attempt to get money from Uncle Benjamin.

Until this point, Digger hadn't felt guilty about not telling Franklin she had found the note and letters. But he might think she should let him know about the potential half-sibling before delving into whatever records she could find at the historical society or maybe the vital records office.

If she could find out what became of the child — or even whether there was a way to do so — she'd bring Franklin on board. If the child couldn't be found, or had died, why add to his angst right now? There would be plenty of time later.

Before she got to the historical society on the town square, Digger turned onto Oak Street and pulled in front of her house. Cameron's truck sat in the driveway and Ed Edison sat on the porch swing. She called to him as she got out of the car. "Comfy, Ed?"

He grinned. "Taking a break. My knees get tired from all the squatting."

She climbed the steps. "I appreciate you doing this on short notice."

"Goes with the territory. I redid the wiring in the bathroom and down that wall. Put in a couple new circuit breakers, but the box itself wasn't that old. Didn't have to replace it."

"Thank heavens for small favors. Cameron inside?"

Ed nodded. "He's close to finishing up. You got anybody to replace your sheet rock?"

"My...? Fix the holes in the wall. No. You volunteering?"

"Nah. Not that good at it and too much to do. Jackrabbit, now, he's developed quite a talent."

Digger grinned. "I didn't think anyone called him that to his face."

"I sure don't. He can do your walls. Probably the kitchen ceiling tiles, too."

She opened the storm door. "Okay. I'll get to him through Cameron." She went into the house and was surprised at how sterile it felt. Compared to the swarm of furniture and overflowing bookshelves of the Ancestral Sanctuary, her house seemed almost barren.

"Cameron?"

He called from down the hall. "Saved me calling you. Check this out."

She winced at the tools on the hallway floor and the coating of repair dust everywhere. She should have shut the doors to the bedrooms. She peered into the bathroom to see Cameron standing in the tub, adjusting the shower head.

"Hey, Digger. I'm checking all the faucets and stuff. Repairs went pretty well upstairs. No surprises beyond what we talked about."

Digger half snorted. "That was enough of a surprise for me."

"Yeah. Charlie, one of the deputies from Sheriff Montgomery's place, stopped by. I told him…"

"Jeez. I told him not to bother."

Cameron frowned. "You didn't file a report?"

She shook her head. "He heard you and me talking on the phone. What did he say?"

"Not much. I showed him the little slits in the pipes I took out, but obviously I'd had my hands all over them. He didn't take them with him."

"It's okay. I just didn't want to give Damion the satisfaction of knowing I had to call the sheriff."

Cameron climbed out of the tub and turned on the shower for a moment, then turned it off. "Works fine."

"Good. I came by to pick up some clothes for the next few days. My pay was deposited today. I'll leave you another check."

"Okay. I may be done by the end of the day."

"Ed said Jackrabbit could do some of the wall repairs. You think he'd be good for that?"

"Yep. He's done it a couple other places where I've had to open up the walls."

They talked about Cameron leaving the key he'd used with Jackrabbit and Digger told him to have him call her so she could arrange to pay him. "When you leave today, could you make sure the shades are down? Probably be people who'll know I'll be up at Uncle Benjamin's for a couple more days."

"Sure. Like the song says, we'll leave a light on for you."

Digger made her goodbyes and drove past the storefront that now housed the historical society. She parked a few doors down and eyed the entrance as she approached it. The society also served as a museum, and the plate glass windows had an eclectic mix of arrowheads, coal miners' hats, and framed photos of some of the earliest buildings in town.

Though the society had been in the building for only a few months, the place already had the smell of musty books and wool fabric, the latter courtesy of donated clothing from the Civil War era. Today what she thought of as the smell of history also combined with that of recent sawdust. Someone must have been adding more bookshelves.

Mrs. Zorn sat at the small desk just inside the building. One of the buildings, since the exhibits were in a recently closed antique store in addition to the former print shop. The owner of the antique store had joined other businesses in a large building near Interstate 68. Uncle Benjamin had told her the man's sales had doubled.

Mrs. Zorn rose and hurried to Digger. "I'm so sorry about Benjamin. He didn't deserve to die that way."

So, the word is out. Digger gently backed out of a firm embrace. The short Mrs. Zorn's permed hair tickled her chin, and her perfume would decimate a beehive. "Thank you. He should have had a lot more years."

"And you found him. How awful."

Digger recognized a hint for information when she heard one. She'd already decided to say only enough to quell rumors. "I did. It seemed he had fallen down the cellar stairs, but I guess the sheriff found evidence that it wasn't an accident."

She bent her head and then looked Digger directly in the eyes. "Hearing he left these two buildings to the historical society was quite a surprise."

"To Franklin and me, too." She didn't add that they hadn't realized he owned them.

When Digger said nothing else, Mrs. Zorn added, "I stopped by the funeral home and they told me when the service would be Saturday. And Doug O'Bannon let us know what food to bring for after."

Digger knew if she didn't find a way to start her research quickly, the conversation could go on for an hour. "That's great. I think I told you I wanted to look for some photos of him, for the display board at the funeral home and house."

Mrs. Zorn sniffed and dabbed at her nose with a tissue. "I have several from our newsletters." She turned to her desk and gestured to a three-ring binder that contained single copies of each newsletter. "I put sticky notes on pages that had his pictures."

Digger stood next to the desk and paged through the binder. She stopped at a photo of him smiling as he cut the ribbon to open the new location. "I like this one." She stood over it and snapped a photo with her phone.

"My goodness, you young people and technology. How will you make a picture from that?"

Digger smiled. "I'll take the memory card from my phone and load these on my computer. Then I'll send them to Walgreens in Frostburg to develop."

"My, my." Mrs. Zorn hovered at her elbow as Digger continued looking. She wanted to remind her that it was still a good idea to stand a few feet from another person. Unconsciously, her eyes strayed to a cloth face mask on the desk.

"Oh, goodness. Since it was you, I forgot to put it on." She adeptly tied it, displaying an image of the American and Maryland flags.

"Nice mask. Since it's been a month since the last case in Garrett County, I forgot and left mine in the car. You want me to get it?"

"No, dear. Unless you've been around a lot of people outside town."

"I haven't." Digger began to think of where she'd been the last few days. The funeral home looked as if it was cleaned hourly, but she had been around Sheriff Montgomery and a couple of deputies, though they sometimes wore masks. And the lawyer. And Cameron and Ed. Cameron always wore a mask. Only two people in Maple Grove had had the virus, and no one for months. If she lived by the interstate, she'd be more concerned.

Digger took two more pictures. She especially liked a shot of him, likely at a historical society board meeting, resting his head on a fist. It accented his square jaw line and prominent cheekbones. His snow-white hair had its semi-mussed look. She smiled. He always thought about so many things and gave little concern to how he looked.

Digger shut the binder. Mrs. Zorn had a single tear coursing down one cheek. She gave a watery smile. "He could be an ornery son-of-a-gun when he wanted his way, but he loved this town."

"He did speak his mind. So, I'd like to look through some older files or articles, maybe get some photos of him and Aunt Clara."

Zorn's expression brightened. "I'd be happy to help…"

Digger shook her head. "If you don't mind, I'd like to look on my own. I loved going through old books with him." Actually, she didn't. She liked to read interesting items he found, but the older documents made her sneeze.

"Of course, dear." Zorn pointed to the chair behind her desk. "I'll be right here if you have any questions."

"Thanks." Digger moved through shelves of history books, family scrapbooks and such to the back of the large room. She placed her purse on one of two wooden tables. She recalled they were solid oak and it had taken four men to carry them. They were older guys, but Digger thought the only duo who could lift them would be a couple of Pittsburgh Steelers linebackers.

She retrieved several Maple Grove High School yearbooks and first looked at Uncle Benjamin's senior year. Captain of the debate team. "I should have known," Digger muttered.

His senior picture showed a handsome young man in a letter sweater. As she flipped through the pages, she saw he had run track. "Huh." *Just like Franklin.*

As she took a few photos of the pictures, Digger realized how few there were of Uncle Benjamin at the Ancestral Sanctuary. Not that she'd expect him to litter the house with his own image, but she could recall only one on display, his and Aunt Clara's wedding photo. Pictures of Franklin and her, plus a few of her parents and sister and family, were arrayed on a wall in the dining room.

Digger glanced toward the front of the room before she checked out Aunt Clara's photos. Her parents had several of her with Uncle Benjamin and Aunt Clara, one of which was taken the weekend before she died.

The sixteen-year old Clara in a yearbook had a broad smile, wavy brown hair, and a locket around her neck. It looked big enough to hold a small picture; Digger didn't think she had seen it. Clara belonged to the pep band and played a trumpet.

Her senior year photo was that of a more somber girl. Very possibly one who knew she was pregnant. Or would she have given up the child by then? Did she try to hide her pregnancy?

In group photos in the back of the yearbook, Clara looked more as she did in the junior class book. Digger studied a photo of a group of kids at the Junior Prom dance. Was Clara holding hands with the handsome boy next to her? It seemed so. Unlike photos of clubs and teams, group photos of dances or other less formal events were not captioned. She took a picture of the prom yearbook photo.

Digger had been at it for half-an-hour. She wanted to get back to the Ancestral Sanctuary to continue to tidy for the funeral dinner. She put the yearbooks on a shelf and headed for the indexes of live births. For the earliest years of Western Maryland settlement, settlement by white people, she reminded herself, these had been compiled from family Bibles and submissions from families, sometimes many years after the fact.

When she and Uncle Benjamin tried to figure out how many children his great-grandmother had, they also went to census records. He didn't know what happened to the oldest family Bible, and verbal family history often didn't include children who died as infants.

In the 1880 census, they found a little girl, age one, named Ella Belle. The entire federal 1890 census had been destroyed in a fire before most states could purchase copies, and Ella Belle was nowhere to be found in 1900. She could have married and moved to California or someplace, but Uncle Benjamin doubted it. He loved it when he found kids who died young, because they should count, too. He had added Ella Belle to the family tree.

Births recorded after 1940 were with the state Vital Statistics Division, but were also in the county of birth. However, there were clear restrictions on who could obtain them, and Digger didn't think the spouse of the birth mother could request it if he wasn't listed as the father on the certificate. Of course, Uncle Benjamin had known people who worked for the county and state governments. He might have been able to get a copy that way. Had he hidden it among his files?

Because Garrett and Alleghany Counties bordered each other, some information was in both historical societies. But neither had birth records, or even indexes later than 1924, which was the most recent date the state made indexes available.

Digger was about to place an older death index on a shelf when she saw a sign on the wall next to it. "The Vital Records Office at the county courthouse will provide birth information to an individual themselves, and for a couple other reasons—which they define. They have a sign that says you can't do a fishing expedition."

To herself, Digger said, "Talk about brick walls." Digger glanced at the time on her phone. Two-thirty. She decided to focus more on photos for Uncle Benjamin's bulletin board, as well as whether she could find out more about Aunt Clara during her senior year of high school.

Digger checked the microfilm indexes for the Maple Grove paper. She could hear Mrs. Zorn stirring as she loaded the microfilm and turned on the machine. To keep her focus on Uncle Benjamin, she first searched for him, and was surprised at the number of articles.

Digger zeroed in on one that announced his enlistment in the Army in 1955 and another about his assignment to Berlin in 1957. She had heard him refer to himself as a peon in the Western Allies' effort to keep the former Soviet Union from gaining control of all of the city.

In the tradition of small-town papers, the two times he came home from Berlin on leave the paper had a brief mention of his visit. He'd worked at the Checkpoint Charlie Crossing that separated the two Berlins, and described how desolate it was on the Eastern side of the city.

In 1960 he returned home for good, just before the Soviets built the wall that separated East and West Berlin. He regretted not being there to "face down the Commies," as US tanks had done at one point in 1961.

The bottom line was that Uncle Benjamin had likely not been in the country when the child was born. Many times Digger had heard the story of Uncle Benjamin spotting Aunt Clara in Maple Grove Malt Shop not long after he returned.

He was intrigued, she was shy, and her parents were horrified that a man seven or eight years older than their daughter was interested in her. They insisted that she complete her teaching degree. She did, and married Uncle Benjamin after teaching for a period of time. Digger didn't know how long.

"Digger?"

She had been so intent on the microfilm that she jumped. "I'm sorry, I didn't hear you."

Mrs. Zorn nodded. "I need to leave in a few minutes. Technically this isn't a day we're open to the public. So…"

"Gosh, I'm sorry if I held you up."

"You didn't. I came in to cut a month's worth of obituaries and wedding announcements out of the paper. Do you want me to leave you a key?"

"No, really. I want to print a couple of these articles about Uncle Benjamin when he was in Berlin, and their wedding article."

"Of course." Mrs. Zorn frowned. "He didn't keep the wedding article?"

"He may have, but it feels odd to go through a lot of his files and all."

"Of course…" she hesitated.

Digger pushed print for the first article. "Eventually I think some of his papers will end up here."

"We can talk about that. He collected a number of books and articles on Maryland history. Maybe a college library would be good for some of them."

"Could be." Digger checked the article that had printed and pressed print for the others. She had another thought about the yearbooks. She didn't have a name for the boy in the Junior Prom photo with Clara, but if he was in the same class he'd have an individual picture.

Mrs. Zorn returned to her desk and Digger went back to the yearbook. She looked at the prom photo again, and then flipped through the junior class individual pictures. And there he was. Gregory Mumsford, class president.

Aunt Clara had always picked top-notch partners.

CHAPTER SEVENTEEN

DIGGER SAID GOODBYE TO Mrs. Zorn and walked to her car. The early afternoon sun had warmed the day. She could almost believe spring was here to stay. As she reached the car, Damion came out of the coffee shop a few doors down.

He wore dress slacks and a colored shirt with a maroon tie. And a big smile. "Beth! Wait up."

She wanted to get in the car and speed off, but knew Mrs. Zorn was nearby and a couple people were on the lawn in front of city hall, across the street. She didn't want to provide fodder for gossip.

Digger stood next to the driver's side door of her car, key in hand. She didn't return his greeting. As he got closer, she said, "Damion, I need to get back to Uncle Benjamin's."

His smile did not fade. "I hear it's your place now."

Digger could feel her cheeks redden. "Where did you hear that?"

"Your uncle's lawyer filed his will. A friend in the courthouse told me you inherited his Ancestral Sanctuary." Damion put the name of the property in air quotes.

Digger pushed the key fob to unlock the car. She had known the probated estate would be a matter of public record, but not necessarily today. She'd love to know who had told him.

"So, Beth, I'm sorry I sounded off yesterday."

"And yet, here you are today. Damion, you need to stop pestering me."

The smile faded and then was back in full wattage. "I know I come on too strong sometimes, but whoever treated you better?"

"We aren't going through this again, Damion. We won't need to see each other at work for probably a good while. Stop thinking about me."

The smile turned to a smug grin. "I'll be at work. They didn't let everyone go you know."

"Good for you." Digger opened her car door and inserted one leg.

"I'll see you at the funeral," Damion said. "Do you need any…"

She put her leg back on the pavement. "I will ask the funeral home staff not to admit you. Don't embarrass yourself by trying to get in." She slid into her seat, pulled the door shut and started the car.

For a moment it seemed he would stand in front of the car so she couldn't pull out of the space. Then he seemed to decide better of it and walked back onto the sidewalk.

Still fuming, Digger stopped at the grocery store to pick up more coffee, cheese blocks to slice, crackers, and two cases of bottled water. She wasn't going to make food for a post-funeral group, but she wanted to have a plate of cheese in the fridge and bowls of crackers on the table to get things started.

As she drove up Crooked Leg Road, Digger had to force herself to concentrate on the curvy trek. But she couldn't. What would it take to get Jerk Damion to stop tracking her? Digger had learned too late that he thought he was the universe's gift to women, but why her? She was attractive but no fashion model, managed her finances well but her only real assets were her house and a small retirement fund. Until now. What was the value of the Ancestral Sanctuary? And why would he care? He seemed to have plenty of money.

She kept going back to the fact that Damion simply wanted what he couldn't control. He should have picked a shy woman who lived with her parents and wanted to get out from under their thumbs. *Probably wouldn't be enough of a challenge for him.*

As she pulled into the driveway, Digger noted that daffodils had popped up in both front flowerbeds. She liked the idea that the yard would be colorful when Uncle Benjamin came through it for the last time.

She parked the Jeep at one edge of the circular driveway. The house might be hers, but when he was home, Franklin had always parked in the circle. She wanted to be sure he still did.

As she removed her two grocery bags from the Jeep, Anna Jean Burke's red Buick turned into the driveway. Digger carried the bags to the front door and went back to shut the SUV's rear hatch.

Maybe if she didn't open the house's front door, Anna Jean would be content to talk on the porch.

Not. She almost leapt from her car and came toward Digger with arms outstretched. Digger picked up a grocery bag of cheese and crackers to use as a shield. "Hello, Ms. Burke."

"Anna Jean, Sugar." She put her arms to her sides. "I'm sorry if I was too forward with you and dear Franklin yesterday." She came up the steps and stood a few feet from Digger.

No mistaking that perfume.

"No problem. It had been a trying day." She briefly took in the muted blues of Anna Jean's outfit. "I hope you're feeling a bit better, too."

Bitsy barked from inside the house. He may have been sleeping in the kitchen when Digger pulled up, but voices had aroused him.

"Did you want to let your dog out, Digger?"

"I probably should." She reached into the pocket of her jacket and took out her keys. She felt cold inside for a moment. This was the first time she'd used the Ancestral Sanctuary key to open the door since Uncle Benjamin died. "You might want to stand back. He'll charge out."

Bitsy did, and Digger let him pass before preceding Anna Jean into the entry hall. She set the bag on the floor. "Come on into the living room."

"Can I help you put anything away?"

"No, I just have a couple of things."

As Digger walked into the room, Ragdoll jumped off the couch and started toward her. The cat took in the two women, turned up her tail, and stalked out of the room. Digger thought she heard a light hiss.

Anna Jean smiled broadly as she sat. "I used to shoo her off the couch. We never did get to be good friends."

"Ah." Digger sat across from her in the same chair she'd sat in to talk to Sheriff Montgomery two nights before. "You said you lived closer to Frostburg. How did you and Uncle Benjamin meet?"

"It's the silliest thing. I'm not into all the history stuff the way he is, but I knew my great grandparents lived in Maple Grove, and I wanted to see if there were any pictures of them."

Digger nodded, trying to look interested.

"So I went to that new society building on the square, and he was volunteering at the desk." She put her palms together, as if praying. "And the rest is history." Her eyes teared. "Or was."

Sorry that she had brought on Anna Jean's tears, and then annoyed with herself for feeling sorry, Digger said, "I wish he'd been able to introduce us."

Anna Jean pressed a finger under each eye.

Perhaps people did this when they didn't want eyeliner running down their cheeks.

"I do, too, Sugar. And we were so close." She sighed and looked toward the fireplace. "We loved sitting in front of the fireplace, holding hands."

Holding hands? She couldn't recall a single photo of Uncle Benjamin and Aunt Clara holding hands. "How long had you been seeing each other?"

Anna Jean tilted her head. "Let's see, almost three months. It may not sound long, but it was the best three months of my life."

Digger smiled, but said nothing. She didn't believe they'd seen each other that long. She would have heard about it.

Anna Jean did an arching gesture with her left hand and arm. "He just loved this house, and I really enjoyed hearing its history."

"Did he give you the cemetery tour?"

Anna Jean did an exaggerated shudder. "Yes. Spooky." She added quickly, "Of course, it was an honor to be introduced to your Aunt Clara."

"I went out there yesterday to tidy up." She glanced at Anna Jean's navy blue sling shoes, with their low heel, and realized she had a way to encourage the woman to leave. "If you have sneakers in the car, you could help me do more."

"Oh, my. I'm afraid these are new. I just came by to..."

A distant car horn beep took their attention to the front window.

Digger stood. A car that Digger figured could be older than she was came up the drive. The fins gave it away as her gossipy neighbor. "One of Uncle Benjamin's friends. Do you know Doug O'Bannon?"

"I believe I've heard the name, but I don't know that we met." Anna Jean picked up her handbag. "I don't want to bother you if one of Benny's good friends is here."

Digger didn't want an extended visit from Anna Jean, but she sensed the woman had come here with a purpose. "He's probably just dropping off some food for after the funeral. He's kind of organizing that."

Anna Jean made for the front door. "I will be at the service. I'd like to come back to the house, too. I could bring some food."

Digger shook her head as she followed the woman. "Just bring yourself."

Anna Jean moved out the front door and down the steps, walking briskly toward her car. She waved to O'Bannon and turned back to Digger. "You take care, Sugar."

O'Bannon's monster car growled to a stop. He lurched out of it and stared at Anna Jean's back for a moment before looking at Digger. "Thought I'd bring by some of the non-perishable stuff and see if you and Franklin needed help."

Digger was beginning to wonder if she would get a chance to look at what she'd brought home from the historical society. "Hello Mr. O'Bannon."

He took a grocery bag from the front seat. "Now, you're all grown up, Digger. Call me Doug."

"Sure thing." She walked down the steps and took the bag from him.

"Just one more. I'll follow you in."

Of course you will. "Can I put this on the dining room table, or does it need to be in the kitchen?"

"Table's fine. Thelma Zorn will be mad at me, but I didn't bring serving dishes for anything. Figured you had plates and all. Some banana bread, made it myself, crackers, soft cookies. Didn't make those." He huffed as he walked up the steps. "We old people need squishy food, you know."

Digger held the door so he could precede her. "You know the way."

O'Bannon glanced into the living room as they passed it. He scanned the dining room as he placed his bag on the table. "I'm not sure what I expected. That it would look different, I suppose."

"It feels it. If you don't mind, I'll unpack this later." She didn't want him hanging around.

"Sure. Nothing will spoil." He faced Digger. "Who was that woman who left a minute ago?"

"Her name's Anna Jean Burke. She and Uncle Benjamin spent some time together."

He sat in a dining room chair and took out a handkerchief to mop his forehead. "Heard about her. Thought they stopped, what was it you said?" He grinned. "Spending time together."

Digger sat next to him. "I didn't get that impression from her." *And she sure had a lot of stuff here for someone he wasn't seeing anymore.*

"Recent split, I thought. Not a split. Just kind of ran its course."

"Did you know her?"

O'Bannon shook his head. "I think he was self-conscious about the age difference." He chuckled. "Course, I never knew your uncle to date anyone his own age."

Digger smiled. "He said they couldn't keep up with him."

After several seconds of silence, O'Bannon looked directly at Digger. "I guess you know all the terms of his will?"

"Franklin and I met with his lawyer, Susan Silver."

"I heard that." He looked away and back again. "He kept a good secret. About the historical society buildings."

The way he left the thought hanging there, Digger thought he was asking a question. "Neither of us knew that he owned them. I heard he, uh, bought them about the time of the move."

O'Bannon nodded. "Caused some hard feelings. Couple of us talked to him about it. Some folks thought he found the buildings and then went after us as tenants."

She regarded him. "I guess some folks are eating their words now."

O'Bannon flushed, then stood. "I'll be on my way. Franklin around?"

"In DC clearing his desk at work. He should be here tomorrow."

"The Browning sense of responsibility. Guess I'll see you both on Saturday."

Digger walked him to the door, accepting without much comment his words about how much he'd miss Uncle Benjamin. She let Bitsy follow him outside, knowing she wouldn't wander because she hadn't eaten much lately.

After she waved him goodbye, she stood in the doorway watching the fins of his car disappear down the drive. She wondered if any of the people eating their words had visited Uncle Benjamin two days ago.

She shook her head to get rid of the thought. Digger realized she wanted to pack up Anna Jean's stuff before Franklin returned. She may have come to retrieve them, but didn't want to with Doug O'Bannon around. Why was that? She didn't want Anna Jean prowling the house after the funeral, looking for her false eyelashes and such.

And she didn't want the bag to become a topic of conversation among the other mourners. Digger would put the bag in her Jeep and they could move it to Anna Jean's car after the funeral.

She used a canvas tote bag to pack the belongings, which she collected from the downstairs bathroom and Uncle Benjamin's bedroom. For good measure, she threw in several books she knew didn't belong to Uncle Benjamin. Two paperbacks had covers with cats sitting on counters in bookstores, and a romance by an author named Leigh Michaels was called *His Trophy Wife*. Maybe that's how Anna Jean saw herself.

As she folded the red sweater that had been on the back of a chair in Uncle Benjamin's bedroom, a coin fell from a pocket. Digger stooped to retrieve it.

Why did Anna Jean have a 1922 silver dollar? Would Uncle Benjamin have given her one of Franklin's special coins?

CHAPTER EIGHTEEN

DIGGER STUDIED THE COIN. This was the 1922 Peace Dollar, which was rare and could sell for several thousand dollars. It couldn't be found in just any coin shop today. Maybe Anna Jean had it and brought it to show Uncle Benjamin. Could that be why the coin boxes were on Franklin's bed? Maybe, but it didn't explain why they were left there.

Digger put the coin in her pocket and took the bag to her SUV and placed it in the back seat. Her presence by the car had roused Bitsy from a doze in the larger of the two flowerbeds. He shook off leaves and small sticks and bounded over.

"Are you having fun being outside without me? No one to tell you not to chase squirrels?" Bitsy looked all around. "You know that word, don't you?"

The dog looked at Digger as if he felt she'd deliberately misled him.

"You want to come in?" Bitsy turned back to the flowerbed.

She reentered the house and went to the living room to open the folder she'd brought home from the historical society. As she spread several items on Uncle Benjamin's desk, Digger realized she was holding her breath. She expelled it and took his well-used magnifying glass from a desk drawer so she could more easily read the muddy quality of documents printed from microfilm.

The wedding article read like the small-town society piece it was. "Miss Clara Forsythe and Mr. Benjamin Browning were united in marriage at the First Methodist Church of Maple Grove on Saturday at four o'clock. The bride was resplendent in a cream satin gown with a train that required the full-time attention of a bridesmaid as Miss Forsythe and her father walked down the aisle."

Digger smiled at the flowery prose. What interested her more was the photo of the bridal party and Clara's parents. At thirty-two, Uncle Benjamin had been without parents for a number of years. Though the article didn't give anyone's age, she thought Aunt Clara had been about twenty-five.

The story mentioned that she had taught elementary school for several years and that Uncle Benjamin was a "well-established local merchant." He had sold the hardware store when Digger was ten.

On Clara's right was a young woman named Agnes Mumsford. Digger looked at one of the photos she had taken at the historical society. As she thought she remembered, that was the last name of Clara's prom date junior year. Had her date (and maybe the baby's father) had a sister who was Clara's good friend? Or was this his wife? He wasn't in the bridal party, so Digger couldn't compare the high school photo to a wedding picture.

Uncle Benjamin's best man was his first cousin, Jefferson Browning. He had been at least ten years older than Uncle Benjamin and died when Digger was in elementary school. At least that's what she'd been told. She had no memory of him. And knowing him wouldn't likely tell her anything about Aunt Clara's baby.

The sound of footsteps on the porch startled Digger and she hastily shoved papers into the folder. She was at the door when the caller knocked. At first, Digger saw no one when she opened the door. Then she realized the person on the porch was a woman barely taller than four feet. She looked familiar, somehow.

Then it clicked. Clara's sister, Eunice. With almost a start, Digger realized Eunice had not been in the bridal party.

Digger opened the storm door. "My goodness. You're Franklin's Aunt Eunice. I'm his cousin, Digger, Beth, Browning."

The woman stared up at her, eyes bright under what appeared to be a perpetual frown. "I certainly know who I am, young lady."

One of the few descriptions she'd heard of Eunice was acid-tongued. She smiled. "No doubt. Please come in."

Eunice brushed past Digger--overlapping long necklaces jiggling against a brightly colored top, accented by a large handbag banging against her hip--into the front hall. She walked toward the back of the house, but stopped at the living room entrance.

"Doesn't look all that different." She sniffed. "I see he still had all his genealogy crap."

Somehow, Digger hadn't expected a woman who was likely in her eighties to swear. "He loved local history." When Eunice kept looking from one item to another, Digger added, "Franklin may not be home this evening. Would you like me to call him to know for sure?"

"I can call my nephew myself."

"Of course." *You old bat.* "Can I offer you some water or tea?"

Eunice faced her, "You can, but I don't need any."

Digger had the impression the woman was trying to figure out if she could steamroll her. Two could play that game. "Okay, then. If you'd like to sit in the dining room with me, I'm going to go through some photos to decide which ones to put on a bulletin board for the funeral home."

Eunice preceded her into the dining room and started to sit in one of the chairs. She quickly rose and there was a plopping noise as Ragdoll jumped to the floor. "Mangy animal," she muttered.

Apparently, the cat had decided to test Digger's reaction. "Go on, Ragdoll. You can cuddle with Bitsy when he comes in."

Eunice sat down. "Do you have old photographs of my family? Benjamin never let me have them."

Warning bells went off. "We might find some. I'm sure Franklin would be willing to make copies for you."

She pointed a finger at Digger. "I want the originals. They were my mother's."

"And then they belonged to Franklin's mother, and if he has kids perhaps someday to them. He can make you copies."

"You're just like your uncle," she snapped.

"Thank you." Digger kept her eyes on Eunice until she turned and looked at her. Then she gave the woman a small smile.

"Humph. I'd like to at least see the originals."

Digger thought it odd that she'd never asked how Franklin was, or said she was sorry about Uncle Benjamin's death. "I'll look for them in a minute. First, I'll show you some of Aunt Clara from high school. But on my laptop, not hard copies."

"You do that."

She took her laptop from the sideboard, opened it, and took the memory card from her phone.

"What are you doing?" Eunice asked.

Digger busied herself with finding and bringing up the photos. "I took pictures of some old photos, including some from Aunt Clara's high school yearbooks. I'll transfer them to my computer, then I can send them to Walgreen's to be printed to put on the bulletin boards at the funeral home."

She opened the folder so she could see small images. "It kind of makes a slide show." She clicked on Aunt Clara's junior year photo.

Eunice leaned forward. "My goodness. It looks just like her." She smiled to herself.

"These aren't all of her, but several are. I can print any of them for you."

Eunice almost spat the words. "I want all the ones of her."

"Sure." Digger moved quickly past the ones of Uncle Benjamin alone. She stopped at any with Clara, and when Eunice said nothing, moved on. She deliberately let the slide show stop again at the prom photo.

Eunice leaned forward. "Who's holding her hand?"

"I looked up his picture in the senior section. His name is Gregory Mumsford."

Eunice's face contorted. "Bastard!"

Digger had an even stronger feeling she was looking at the father of Clara's baby. "We can move on. Why do you, uh, not like him?"

"That's my business. I don't want that one." She looked closely at Digger. "Why were you getting pictures of my sister from before she married Benjamin?"

"I went to the historical society to look for some of Uncle Benjamin, but then I thought Franklin might like some of his mother, too."

The next photo was the wedding article. "I can take out just the picture and then enlarge it, if you like."

Eunice stared at the article for several seconds. "Who's the bridesmaid on the far right?"

Though she knew, Digger pretended to try to decipher the name from the small caption. "Agnes Mumsford."

In a kind of sing-song tone, Eunice said, "The bastard's bride."

"I take it you don't want that one…" The phone interrupted her. "Just a second."

Digger walked the few steps to the kitchen and answered the house phone. She turned to nod at Eunice as she did so. Let Ms. Acid-Tongue know she didn't plan to let her out of her sight.

"Hello? Mom? Have your plane reservation yet?" Digger listened for almost thirty seconds. "No, really, I get it. You can call tomorrow and talk to Franklin."

Eunice glanced around the dining room, but Digger could tell she was paying attention to the conversation. "Sure, Mom. You'll never guess who's here. Franklin's Aunt Eunice."

Her mother's voice rose an octave. "In Benjamin's house? Eunice?"

Digger smiled at Eunice. "Yes, Mom, right here. Would you like to speak to her?"

Eunice waved a hand in front of her face and shook her head.

Her mother lowered her voice. "I'm sorry. Did she hear me?"

"Nope."

"Your uncle never let her wander. He said she wanted a brooch Clara's mother had."

"I get that," Digger said. "How about I call you later tonight?"

After listening to her mother tell her she loved her and knew how much she would miss Uncle Benjamin, Digger hung up. She went back to the table. "My parents were going to fly up from Florida, but they decided it still isn't a good idea to be on a plane. I guess they'll drive up to see Franklin another time."

Eunice studied her for a moment. "Your father was Thomas."

"Yes, Uncle Benjamin was actually his unc…"

"I know that." She pointed to the wedding article. "I want that, too."

"Okay." Digger sat next to her again. "Would you want to know how Franklin is?"

Eunice looked at a couple points in the room and then at Digger. "I don't have his phone number."

"I'll write it down before you go. He's doing pretty well. Sad, of course, so am I."

"Mmmm. Guess he'll be pretty rich now, won't he?"

Digger wasn't about to have a detailed discussion of finances with the woman. But if Silver had filed the will, it might have been made public. "He likes his work as a lawyer in DC. I doubt his life will change much."

Eunice slapped the table with the palm of her hand. Hard. "That man got his start with my sister's money!"

Digger couldn't help herself. "What do you mean?"

"When Clara left her teaching job, she worked with him in that stupid hardware store. Took her retirement money out of her teachers' fund, and he invested it."

Digger flushed. "Married people often have joint finances."

"That's what she said. So gullible."

Digger stood. "Let me write down the house phone number. That would be best for Franklin."

"I need his cell phone number."

"I planned to give it to you, but since you were so rude about Uncle Benjamin, I'll let Franklin decide if he wants you to have it."

Eunice stared at Digger, then laughed. "I like you."

"Perhaps later I can say the same."

Eunice laughed again. Then sobered. "Would you walk me out to the graves?"

That caught Digger off guard. "Sure."

Eunice stood and took a folding cane from her handbag and popped it open. "I don't use this indoors."

"Good idea for the yard here. It's lumpy. You're welcome to leave your purse in here."

In a less frosty tone, Eunice said, "I'll do that. I'd like to go to the bathroom first." She picked up her purse, but left her cane lying across the table.

"Sure." Digger stayed seated. She signed onto her Walgreen's account and uploaded the photos she wanted to order. There would be more later, but she went ahead and ordered two prints of everything she had made copies of.

As she pushed the button noting she would pay at the store in Frostburg, the toilet flushed and the door to the little bathroom opened. Digger stood and plastered a pleasant expression on her face.

Eunice entered the dining room. "I'm ready." She retrieved her can from the tabletop.

Digger walked through the kitchen and held open the back door so Eunice could precede her down the back porch steps. "I was out there earlier today clearing away winter sticks and brush."

They walked about halfway to the plot in silence. Eunice stopped and turned to stare at the house. "Clara made his old wreck a home."

Digger suppressed a giggle. She'd seen lots of pictures of the house in its heyday. Gorgeous, beautifully furnished, stunning would all be appropriate adjectives.

Eunice turned around and trudged on. "You think Franklin will keep it?"

"If you saw the will at the Oakland Courthouse, then you know I inherited it."

"What makes you think I saw the will?"

"You mentioned that Uncle Benjamin left Franklin some money. I don't know that he talked much about his assets."

Eunice sniffed. "Will you keep it?"

"Yes. Now I have a question for you."

"What's that?"

"I barely remember Aunt Clara. And neither one of them were fresh out of high school when they married. What was she like? What kinds of things had she done before she married Uncle Benjamin?"

For a second Eunice's stern expression softened, but not for long. "I didn't see her as much after, well after she got out of high school. I was older and had already left home."

"Ah. But you were around some after Franklin was born, I think."

They had reached the arched entry.

She nodded. "Those were good years. Though Benjamin didn't like me. I could tell."

"I'm sorry." Digger nodded ahead of her. "Would you like a moment alone at Aunt Clara's grave?"

Eunice's strident tone softened. "Yes, I would." Making little use of the cane, she moved toward it.

Digger picked up a few more sticks and threw them beyond the edge of the little cemetery. She wanted to feel charitable toward Eunice, but it was impossible. What she wanted more was to know if Eunice knew anything about a baby born roughly sixty years ago. How could she bring that up?

The sound of a car door closing made Digger turn toward the house.

"Eunice. Someone just drove up. I'm heading inside for a minute."

"No, wait. I'm ready." She leaned on her cane as she made her way toward Digger.

Digger didn't want to wait. She'd left the front door unlocked. Uncle Benjamin often left it like that when he was home, but today had been the wrong time to do it. She could almost hear Sheriff Montgomery ask, "And did you let the burglar in through the unlocked front door?"

"Okay, but if we can hustle a little. I want to see who's here."

Eunice picked her way slowly across the uneven grass. "Maybe it's Franklin."

"Don't think so." Digger tried to keep impatience from her voice. "I shouldn't have left the front door unlocked."

When they got to the house, Digger walked up the back porch steps and opened the door to call, "Be right there."

Footsteps came quickly toward them from the front hallway. Anna Jean Burke's voice responded. "Okay, Sugar. I've been making myself at home."

CHAPTER NINETEEN

DIGGER TOLD HERSELF SHE couldn't explode. *How dare the woman just walk into Uncle Benjamin's house?*

As Anna Jean grew closer, she did a hundred-watt smile. "I knocked. I saw cars out front, so I knew you were still here, Digger." She stopped when she saw Eunice. "Oh my, you have company."

Digger ushered Eunice in ahead of her and, for a change, her tongue didn't wag.

She stepped behind the elderly woman to shut the screen door. "Anna Jean Burke, this is Clara's sister, Eunice."

The tongue revived. "Who are you? Did you know my sister?"

"Why no, Benny and I…"

Digger pointed beyond the kitchen. "Let's have a seat in the living room."

Anna Jean chattered as they went. "Now if you're Clara's sister, you know all about Benny and this wonderful old house."

Digger would have sworn she saw tendrils of smoke rising from Eunice's ears. "Anna Jean is this a social call or did you want to pick up your things?"

Eunice almost snapped her neck turning toward Digger. "She has *things* here?"

Digger ushered them both into the living room. She sat in the chair across from the couch, and the other two sat across from her, at opposite ends of the couch.

It would be hard to imagine two more different women. Anna Jean wore her usual trendy clothes — deep mauve rather than hot pink — while the diminutive Eunice's floral pantsuit would bring a pretty penny in a vintage store.

Before she spoke, Digger remembered that Doug O'Bannon had said he thought Anna Jean and Uncle Benjamin had stopped dating not long before his death. But she couldn't exactly say that, so she said, "Eunice, Anna Jean and Uncle Benjamin were close friends."

Anna Jean's laugh would not have been deemed dignified. "I'll say we were."

Eunice thumped her cane on the floor and stood. "I'll get my purse and leave."

"Well now," Anna Jean began.

Digger silenced her by raising a finger, and followed Eunice into the dining room. "I'll let Franklin know you came by."

She picked up her purse. "I want those pictures."

"Will you be at the funeral?"

She stopped. "When is it?"

"Saturday, at the funeral home. I can write…"

"I'll call them." With no trace of a limp or slow walk, Eunice marched down the hall and swept out of the house.

Digger stood in the hallway watching Eunice walk down the front steps, then turned to go back into the living room and almost bumped into Anna Jean. "Oh my God."

Anna Jean backed up. "I'm sorry, Sugar. I mean about scaring you and maybe running her off. I went into town, and then thought I'd come back to see about my things."

"No big deal." Digger started for the front door. "I have a bag with your things in my SUV."

Anna Jean stood still. "Oh. Are you sure you got everything?"

Digger turned to face her and forced a smile. "Anything that was in sight or in an obvious place. Did you have any personal belongings somewhere else?"

Anna Jean adopted what appeared to be a thinking pose. "Well now, I don't think so."

"How about this? We'll put the bag in your car, you can go through it this evening. If something isn't there, you'll be here after the funeral. I'll help you find it then."

"Are you busy now?"

Digger didn't owe this woman any explanation. "Yes." But she gave one anyway. "I have my laptop, and I need to finish a project for work." Certainly not true.

With obvious reluctance, Anna Jean followed Digger to her SUV and accepted the bag of her belongings.

AFTER TEN MINUTES OF cooling off mentally and with a glass of iced tea, Digger strode around the first floor trying to see it as a post-funeral luncheon guest would. She thought Uncle Benjamin's research folders should be moved out of the living room, and assumed Franklin would agree.

She would have to tell him about Anna Jean's and Eunice's visits — two for Anna Jean — so he'd know what to expect if they showed up again. If her mother was right about Eunice wanting jewelry, Franklin needed to be prepared to tell her she wasn't getting it. Although he might feel differently.

She wandered back to Uncle Benjamin's desk and turned on the computer that held his family history files and a database of ancestors, descendants, and a few people he called shirttail cousins. He described them as people who were not relations but were perhaps family of in-laws or had some other connection.

The desktop computer showed its age with a slow start-up. The contents were not password-protected, so Digger went right to his database. With a start, she saw he had added an entry under Aunt Clara — a first spouse and child, but each was named "unknown.". Digger knew the ancestry program didn't let him designate a woman (or man) as an unmarried parent. Old-fashioned sensibilities he called the practice.

Though he had the references, Uncle Benjamin had no more information than was in his file. However, he had some research notes. He'd found the same records Digger had located in the historical society, but he'd also searched marriage records for several women Aunt Clara's age. Perhaps high school friends. And there it was. Agnes Barnes had married Gregory Mumsford several years before Uncle Benjamin and Clara married.

Uncle Benjamin knew them, of course, but did he suspect that Gregory Mumsford had fathered a child with Aunt Clara? Did he know?

Digger checked the Social Security Death index and found that Mumsford had died almost a year ago. She knew it was the same man because of his birth year and the fact that he died in a hospital in Frostburg. Not proof positive, but good enough for now.

Digger added his birth and death information to Uncle Benjamin's database, and saved his information to Uncle Benjamin's ancestry.com family tree. She didn't show him as related to anyone on the tree, but did add his wife's name. Did Agnes know her husband may have fathered a child before their marriage?

Digger pushed herself back from the computer. Conjecture, that's all she had. But conjecture supported by Eunice Forsythe's intense reaction to Mumsford. Of course, Eunice probably harbored a number of grudges and dislikes.

Most of the information Digger found had been provided in other researchers' family trees. The Mumsfords' names appeared only because they were dead. Otherwise the other trees would have listed 'private' for living people.

None of this helped Digger decide if she should report what she found to Franklin right away. Ultimately, she would, but not right before his father's funeral.

She switched to the Ancestry DNA segment in Uncle Benjamin's account. He had distant cousins all over the place, and a few close relatives, including Digger and her father.

But Aunt Clara had died long before genealogy DNA kits. If only Franklin had submitted his DNA. It might show links to unexpected people. Uncle Benjamin had asked him to do it several times, had even bought a kit and given it to him so Franklin could mail in a tube of saliva. But that was a while ago. Digger bet he wouldn't do so today.

Franklin did not have an Ancestry account, so Uncle Benjamin would have technically been the 'manager' of Franklin's DNA results. Since the information was not there, it meant Franklin hadn't submitted the swab for evaluation.

She ran fingers through her hair. All she really had was the odd handwritten letter that Uncle Benjamin received. The lawyer's letters, too, but they were all simply assertions.

Speculation would have to wait a few days. She turned off the computer. After staring at the two stacks of research folders, she decided to take them to the attic. Franklin would not touch them over the next few days, and she didn't want anyone else going through them. If he said he wanted them down here now, she'd retrieve them.

Digger grabbed a couple of dust rags from under the kitchen sink and took the pile of family folders upstairs first. Then she went back down for the Garrett County and Maryland piles. When all three sat at the foot of the stairs, she opened the door to the attic. She sat each on a step and then shut the door behind her and climbed the stairs.

Today the temperature was perfect. Though not an ideal place for historic preservation, a window air conditioner kept the room below eighty degrees in the summer. Uncle Benjamin had cut a square in the floor and brought one duct from the house's heating system into the attic. While it didn't keep the space toasty, he'd also had an electrician install a double outlet near the top of the stairs. If the temperature dropped too low in the winter, he'd plug in a portable heater that looked like an old-fashioned radiator. Less risk of fire than other heaters, he said.

Digger surveyed the large room. Uncle Benjamin had built shelves into the eaves, where the sloping roof made it impossible to stand. On them were varied size boxes. Aunt Clara had labeled some of them with things like "Franklin's Baby Clothes" and "My mother's cookbooks." That flowery handwriting was on only a few boxes. The rest had Uncle Benjamin's block letters and said things such as "Maryland pioneers" and "Photo Albums."

Across from the head of the stairs sat a large table of molded plastic that she'd helped Franklin haul up here several years ago, as a joint Father's Day gift. Franklin had read an article about how concurrently bending and reaching was bad for a person's back, and he didn't want his father bending over boxes so much.

Digger rarely came to the attic. She smiled remembering that while Uncle Benjamin had appreciated the table, he'd confided to her that it would mostly be a "dust catcher." She took a rag she'd placed in her waistband, dusted the table, and put the piles of folders on it. Then she took the box of photo albums from its spot on the shelves and placed it on the table.

The five albums were a mix of older photos of the Forsythe and the Browning families, one each of Aunt Clara and Uncle Benjamin before they married. One album had a few pictures of them before Franklin was born, but mostly dozens of his younger life. The album ended at roughly the time of her death. Apparently, Uncle Benjamin hadn't wanted to continue the practice. Digger did some mental calculations. Digital photos had also come into vogue. He had a bunch of photos on his computer.

Digger picked up the Browning album. Uncle Benjamin had scanned it years ago, so she'd seen the photos, but not the album itself. She thumbed through it. His square jaw was evident in several men and a couple of women, and was especially noticeable in pictures before about 1870. Exposure time was so long that people couldn't hold a smile, so they all had serious expressions. And probably bad teeth they didn't want to show.

The Forsythe family didn't arrive in the U.S. until the 1880s, and it appeared they didn't bring any photos with them from Ireland. Aunt Clara had labeled birth and death dates for each person. Because she was the youngest of her parents' children and had had Franklin later in life, both sets of her grandparents died before he was born.

Her parents clearly delighted in their grandson. Digger studied the dates for Clara's parents. She hadn't realized they were in their early seventies when he was born. One had died when he was ten and the other when he was thirteen. At least they didn't live long enough to see their youngest daughter die.

The several photos of Clara and Eunice were studies in contrasts. Clara always bore a wide smile, and the best Eunice seemed able to do was a prim one that showed no teeth. But they appeared to have gotten along as girls. They had linked arms for several photos. In the earliest ones after Clara was born Eunice appeared to delight in the baby.

Clara put in dates only for those who had died, so Digger didn't know Eunice's precise age. She looked to be six years older than Clara, which would put her in her eighties now. Clara had few pictures of Eunice after she was perhaps eighteen. That made sense. At that point in their lives, the age difference would have kept them from spending a lot of time together. Or Eunice could have left home to work or go to school.

Digger turned a page and almost gasped. When Clara looked to be sixteen or seventeen, she and Eunice stood on either side of a lilac bush, with the bush obscuring part of each sister. From the weight gain in Clara's face, Digger bet she was pregnant.

Another photo showed the girls — Clara and the adult Eunice — lying on the floor, smiling at the camera, with only heads and shoulders visible. That and other photos from the same time period were not taken in their parents' well-appointed home. Walls bore no paintings and the furniture seemed shabby. Had Clara gone to some kind of home for unwed mothers? Their parents did not appear in any photos at that time. Did they know Clara was pregnant? Had they sent her away?

When she turned the page again, Digger almost dropped the album. Eunice held a tiny baby, and the photo was captioned, "Eunice with her good friend's new baby." Eunice appeared entranced by the tiny bundle of indeterminate sex. In a black-and-white photo, not even the blanket the child was wrapped in could offer a hint. The album held no photo of Clara with the child.

Digger felt certain Eunice held Clara's baby. She must have stayed with her sister, or been nearby, during that summer. Digger could tell the season because lilacs had been in the earlier photo — a spring flower — and a vase on a table near Eunice and the baby held zinnias and dianthus — a summer bouquet.

Given the timing, Clara might have been able to hide her pregnancy from her classmates. Maybe even her parents. She had had a solid build. Unless the baby protruded like a basketball, Clara could have hidden it in bulky clothing until the last few months. When she might have gone away with Eunice.

What happened to the baby? The more she thought about it the less likely it seemed Uncle Benjamin had known. Maybe no one but Eunice knew. And the father. And whoever sent the note to Uncle Benjamin not long before he died.

CHAPTER TWENTY

AT SIX O'CLOCK, DIGGER LEFT the albums in the attic and returned to the first floor to make a sandwich. She'd been so preoccupied she hadn't eaten lunch. Just as she opened the refrigerator the phone rang.

"Digger? Sheriff Montgomery here."

"Hello, Sheriff."

"Franklin still not home?"

"I'd bet on tomorrow afternoon, could be evening."

"Humph. Don't want to wait that long. I have his cell."

"Am I allowed to hear what you've got?"

Montgomery hesitated. "I've no problem with that. Let's see." He shuffled papers. "Initial toxicology report showed Benjamin's usual medicines, which were few. What we expected."

"That's good, I guess."

"Reinforces that he didn't take anything that might affect balance, so he likely didn't trip on the stairs. Lots of latent fingerprints. Yours were on file because you did some substitute teaching when you first got out of college. Benjamin's from his military service."

"How many others?"

"Several. I'm going to have to ask some of the regulars at the house, like your buddy Anna Jean, for comparison prints. Franklin, too. Anyone else there regularly?"

"Let's see. Damion was here a few times, but not for more than a month. Uncle Benjamin mostly did his own housekeeping, but a few times a year he had a woman from town help. Marcia…Marcella."

"I know who you mean. I can get hers."

"I'm sure you checked this, but were there prints near the answering machine? From when someone took the tape?"

"Just yours and his. Seems like the eject button was wiped off."
More paper shuffling. "Not a lot more on cause of death. The fall
down the steps didn't help him, but Cluster and Parker believe
there was a blow to the head from a different angle. Probably
dazed him, and then he went down."

Digger shuddered. "Ugh."

Sheriff Montgomery grunted. "He was a good man. Didn't
deserve to go that way."

She kept thinking she wanted to ask him something else. Then
it clicked. "Did, uh, was Damion able to account for his time
Monday afternoon?"

"Pretty much. Left work not long after you did. Stopped by
your place, as you know, went to the grocery store. Had a receipt.
Didn't have any real reason to suspect him."

After a pause, Digger asked, "Do you think you'll find
who did it?"

"Eventually. No one noticed any unusual cars that afternoon,
but all the houses along there are set back from the road. We
won't give up."

"I know you won't. Thanks." Digger hung up and walked to
the door that led to the back porch. From there she could see the
outline of the small cemetery plot. She hated that from now on
Uncle Benjamin would be there.

Digger checked with Cameron, who said Jackrabbit would
start on her walls the next day and he'd given him the key to her
house. "If you want to pass on any particular instructions, I'd say
come by about seven-thirty tomorrow morning."

After she hung up, Digger stared around the kitchen. She didn't
feel hungry, but breakfast had been a long time ago. Hungry or
not, she had to eat something.

She made a grilled cheese sandwich and rummaged in Uncle
Benjamin's vegetable drawer in the fridge. Broccoli, carrots, and
celery. The broccoli needed to be eaten soon, so she put it on a
shallow plate in the microwave.

She let Bitsy in, but because she didn't want to share her meal,
she put food in Bitsy's bowl and pointed to it when she sat down
to eat her sandwich. He didn't usually eat at this time, but when

he saw his bowl, he stuck his snout in it and began to chomp. She put a few pieces of dry food in Ragdoll's bowl, knowing the cat would show up when she pleased.

She finished her sandwich and called Franklin.

"Hey, Digger. I was about to call. You okay?"

"As okay as I can be. Did Sheriff Montgomery get you?"

"Franklin sighed. "Yes. Makes it seem more real yet more unbelievable."

When he said nothing more, she said, "I've been gathering photos of your dad for a display at the funeral home."

"I've got one in my wallet I like. But I don't want to lose it."

"I'll take a picture of the original and send it to Walgreens with some others." After a pause of several seconds, she asked, "Do you know your timing yet?"

"I think I can finish up tonight. I'm suddenly so tired I can barely stand up."

"Reaction to everything, maybe. You at your office?"

"Just left. I'm walking back to my place and I'll probably be in bed by eight o'clock."

"You had a long day." She hoped if he left early tomorrow he'd be home when the people came to dig Uncle Benjamin's grave.

"Hope so, but I'm not setting an alarm. Everything okay up there?"

"Yes. I put little nails in the windows. The big surprise was your Aunt Eunice showed up."

The phone got so quiet Digger wondered if she'd lost the connection.

"That's…surprising. Sheriff Montgomery offered to find her phone number for me. She and Dad hadn't spoken in years, so I told him I'd wait until after the funeral."

"She probably still knows people in town." Through the phone Digger heard the sounds of city traffic. She hoped Franklin was paying attention as he walked.

"Is she coming to the funeral?"

"She didn't commit. Said she'd check with the funeral home." Digger hesitated. "She also said she wants your mom's photo albums. I told her they were yours and you would be willing to make her copies of any photos she wanted."

"Good. I don't…dislike her. She just hasn't been part of my life since right after mom died. She really hated Dad for some reason. I'm surprised she showed up."

"She wanted your cell, and I told her she'd been kind of rude so I wouldn't give it to her, she could call the house."

"I bet that went over well."

"She told me I was like your dad. I thanked her."

"Good for you."

Digger mentioned the pictures she'd found at the historical society and the visit from the reporter.

"Hofstedder. Don't think I know him."

"His grandparents are the Wilsons. I didn't give him your number, but he'll probably look for you."

"Sorry you have to run interference. Listen, I'm almost home. I may call back this evening, but if I go to bed really early, I won't."

"Okay, but I have one more question."

"Sure."

"Was one of your coins the 1922 peace silver dollar?"

"I did have that one. I bet it was in the box I marked so cleverly."

Digger did a half-grunt, half-giggle. "I found one in your dad's room. I think it fell out of a pocket of something that belonged to Anna Jean."

"You think?" Franklin asked.

"I pretty much know. I collected her things from around the house, to give to her. It fell out of a pocket."

"Jeez." After a pause, he said, "I suppose Dad could have showed it to her, but it's not at all likely. I don't know that he ever went through my stuff. He might not have known I had it."

"There's one way we'll find out."

"What's that?"

"If it was hers and she thinks she lost it, she'll ask if I found it. If she was stealing it, she'll never ask."

"Good observation, Detective Browning."

"Funny." She signed off and grabbed a broom from the kitchen to sweep the front porch. Uncle Benjamin said he kept the house clean by doing a little bit of work every day. Right now, it looked like a gargantuan task.

THURSDAY MORNING, DIGGER WOKE to the sound of machinery in the yard. Uncle Benjamin paid someone to mow the large area around the house, but the grass hadn't grown that much since the last mowing.

Then she remembered the gravediggers. The window in the guest bedroom — she couldn't think of herself as the owner yet — faced the graves. A small backhoe sat at the end of the side driveway, and the large truck that had deposited it sat belching smoke from its tailpipe.

Digger grabbed a pair of jeans and pulled on the shirt she had worn yesterday and ran down the stairs. *So much for Franklin being here when they started to work on the grave.*

As she got to the bottom of the steps someone pounded on the front door. She opened it to see a short man who looked familiar, but didn't think she really knew him. Lots of people were of medium build with graying hair and a broad face.

"Ms. Browning? I'm Don Phelps from the town cemetery? We're contracted to open Mr. Browning's grave for the burial tomorrow?"

For a minute Digger thought he was asking her if that was his job, but then she realized he was just talking in upspeak. "Yes. I wasn't sure when you were coming. Give me a minute to put on work boots and I'll be right out."

The man said nothing, but turned and walked toward his truck.

Digger shut the door, but made for the kitchen first. She'd filled the coffee maker last night and pushed the button for it to brew. God knows, she'd need coffee for this.

Five minutes later she walked out the back door and joined Mr. Phelps on the side yard.

"I never did a grave out here. Guess it's been a long time since one was dug?"

"Yes, my aunt's. The stone is there, so I guess you have to move it to dig the second grave. I'll go up with you, but if you don't mind, I won't watch you dig."

"Fine by me. I been looking at the layout? Other graves here were dug by hand, but we don't do that anymore? I think I can get this little backhoe up there without damaging any stones."

Thankfully, he had turned off his truck and now turned the key in his backhoe. It sort of chugged the distance between the house and the graves. Digger followed him, easily keeping pace.

Phelps stopped at the edge of the grave area. "Tell me it isn't the big one."

"I'm afraid it is. Is that a problem?

Phelps shook his head. "I gotta get somebody else up here with a tripod hoist. If it was one of those old stones, I could rig up some rope and a harness myself." He pointed to a bundle on the floor by his feet."

"You should be able to get a cell signal. You want some coffee?"

For the first time Phelps smiled. "With milk."

Digger entered the kitchen from the back door and studied Bitsy, who sat under the Formica table. "You aren't scared of the backhoe, are you? You like the garbage truck when it comes by at our house."

She took Phelps his coffee in a previously used Starbucks cup — which Uncle Benjamin always maintained he washed out well. As she warmed her own coffee, Phelps' truck belched as it backed onto the main drive. "Ragdoll. The truck's gone. Come down here." She waited ten seconds. "Okay, stay hidden."

Yesterday Digger had been so absorbed in the photo albums that she hadn't taken digital pictures of any of them. She decided to bring downstairs the one with the photos of Clara and Eunice and young Franklin with his parents.

As she trudged up to the attic, Digger again considered whether she should tell Franklin what she knew. Now that Eunice had appeared, she decided she couldn't wait until after the funeral. Who knew what the rude woman would blurt out? Wait. *Did Eunice send the handwritten note about a baby?*

Digger pondered that as she carried the albums down the short flight of steps and placed them on a small table on Uncle Benjamin's room, which was across from the attic. She shut the attic door and turned to retrieve the heavy albums.

The door to Uncle Benjamin's closet stood halfway open. Perhaps Franklin had looked in there before he left for DC.

Digger thought back to night Uncle Benjamin died, when a person had been in the kitchen when she was upstairs in bed. Had they come back? *That's ridiculous.*

She crossed the room and stood outside the small walk-in closet. Along the back wall was a small trunk, and on top of that sat and Clara's jewelry box. Digger had been allowed to look in it as a small child, but not to touch anything.

The lid on the jewelry box was open. Franklin could have looked in there, but Digger felt certain he would have shut it. She thought Eunice hadn't been in the house other than the time she was there with Digger. Besides, the woman would have trouble making it up the steps. Anna Jean Burke had been in the house several minutes before Digger and Eunice returned from the graves. She certainly could have opened it.

Digger slapped herself on the forehead. Did Anna Jean have a key? Digger walked the few paces to the box and looked in it. There was no obvious empty space where purloined jewelry had been. But that didn't mean much.

She was usually a decisive person, but right now Digger wasn't sure what to do. She really had no basis for calling the Sheriff's office. Still, she felt spooked. When Franklin came home, she needed to ask him if he remembered leaving the closet open. She shut the lid on the jewelry box and left the closet.

Digger plopped the photo albums on the dining room table, looked around the dining room, and then walked into the kitchen. She was going to have to get used to being in a large house by herself.

She returned to the dining room and began carefully taking pictures of the photos in the album. She had to stand directly over them and move as close as she could, still keeping them in focus. She took several of the one of Eunice holding the baby. Even when she turned on the close-up feature on her phone's camera, she couldn't see the baby's face. Not that it would tell much.

She again removed the card from her phone, placed it in her laptop, and sent the pictures to Walgreens. That finished, she debated whether to take the albums back to the attic again, but decided not to. However, she didn't want to leave them where Eunice would see them, so she hauled them back to her room. She would let Franklin know where to find them.

Phelps still hadn't returned with a helper, so she turned on Uncle Benjamin's computer again. She wanted to see find out about Mumsford. He had lived in the area presumably all his life. Did he and his wife socialize with Uncle Benjamin and Clara? Did they have children? She had found his death information but had not looked for an obituary.

It didn't take long to find one. He had operated an independent insurance agency in Oakland, the county seat. Her eyes grew wide. He and Agnes had one son who had died about fifteen years ago. The obituary mentioned a grandson, but did not name him.

Did that grandson do a DNA test and realize he had more relatives somewhere? Digger wished there were a way to find out who had sent DNA samples to Ancestry. Or one of the other DNA companies. But there would be privacy issues. She knew from her own test and its results that people had a choice of whether to make their data, or their name, public, but there would be no public access to lists of submitters.

Digger turned off the computer. She had focused on Clara's prom date as the father because that was her only clue. She had become like the person whose only tool was a hammer. Every problem became a nail.

She stood to stretch.

Someone pounded on the back door and she returned to the kitchen. Digger had been so intent on what she was doing she had not heard Phelps' truck return.

He stood there with a younger man behind him. She unlatched the door, but they didn't enter. Phelps shifted his weight from one foot to the other, kind of like a kid in trouble. "See, it's not a very big crack."

For a minute, Digger didn't understand. Then she did. Her voice rose an octave. "The headstone has a crack?"

"Just in the back?"

"And it's not very big," the other man said.

Digger took him in. The broken veins in his otherwise youthful face indicated a familiarity with spirits beyond those in a cemetery. "Is it in the front or the back?"

"Back," both men said.

"Can it be fixed before tomorrow?" Digger asked.

They both shook their heads. "But it's on the back," Phelps said. "The marker will be under a tarp tomorrow? Then when Mr. Browning's dates are added, they can use some granite epoxy to fix it."

Digger blew her lips in a sigh. "We can't do anything now. I'll tell his son when he gets home."

"I'm Stan, by the way. I know Franklin. You can tell him I'll be sure it's fixed right."

"Are you done digging?"

"Just starting. Have to finish and cover the dirt with a tarp, case it rains," Phelps said.

"You guys want something to drink before I head out?" Digger had no plans to leave, but she couldn't deal with two bumbling guys anymore.

"No ma'am," both said.

She shut the door before they turned to leave the porch.

CHAPTER TWENTY-ONE

AS DIGGER WALKED FROM the kitchen to dining room, the house phone rang. She returned to the kitchen and answered it.

"Ms. Browning? Marty Hofstedder here."

Caution crept into her tone. "Good morning. And it's Digger."

"Digger. Again, I'm sorry about your uncle."

"Thanks."

"I haven't been able to get hold of your cousin. Could I ask you a couple more questions?"

She didn't feel like talking, but she had liked the reporter with the bumbling air. There were few enough people her age in town, and he looked like someone who could hang around with her and Holly and a couple others from work.

"You can ask, but I can't think of any I would answer."

Humor entered his tone. "That's because you haven't heard them yet."

Digger smiled. "Fair enough. What's up?"

"You can imagine that people all over town are talking about this. Your uncle sold the hardware store a long time ago, but almost anyone older than twenty-five knew him."

"True. But that's a statement, not a question."

He chuckled. "That was my lead-in. Some people say he could be ornery, but other than that dust-up at the historical society last year — and that's called water under the bridge — no one was angry with him."

"Still no question."

"Several people have mentioned that he had some valuable antiques. Couple people remembered Franklin had a coin collection, because he won a ribbon at the State Fair. Was anything missing?"

The colonial pitcher flashed through Digger's mind. She'd forgotten about it. "Probably not."

"Probably is one of those words that make reporters keep looking."

She couldn't go to a bunch of antique stores and ask about the pitcher. Aside from her questions starting tongues wagging, she had no time. "The thing is, an item or two aren't where they were, but if a thief wanted to burglarize the place, there are probably dozens of other things to take first." Like his wallet, computer, big-screen TV.

"Like what?"

Digger paused. "I don't really know you. Maybe when you deal with people you charge ahead like Pickett at Gettysburg."

"Give me a chance to be discreet," Hofstedder said.

"Okay. The computer and TV were here, obvious items for a thief. But in his bedroom, Uncle Benjamin had a pitcher from colonial times. It sat on an antique washstand."

"And it's gone?"

"Seems to be. But he could have given it away."

"Did he give away a lot of antiques?" he asked.

"No. Have you heard anything about break-ins on the mountain?"

Hofstedder spoke slowly. "No. But I could look around for the pitcher."

She had hoped he would say that. "Where would you look? Antique stores?"

"There, pawn shops, Craigs List, eBay. Do you have any pictures of it?"

"There could be pictures in Uncle Benjamin's safe deposit box at the bank…"

"You haven't looked there yet? Maybe he left a note or something, in case anything happened to him."

Digger smiled. "You read a lot of mystery books?"

"No, but I like to ferret out information. You want to look together?"

"Franklin would be the person to ask. But there won't be any clues about what happened to him."

"Ye of little faith. Tell me about the pitcher. Was is white?"

She called its image to mind. "Kind of off-white. Maybe white at first. And someone had painted some small buttercups on one side. I doubt they were on it when the pitcher was thrown."

"Thrown?"

"By a potter. They say that instead of 'made.'"

"The buttercups are good. I'll let you know what I find out about the pitcher." Hofstedder hung up.

His questions made her think about the safe deposit box, and then whether the deed for the property could be there. She called Samantha Silver.

"I believe the deed is in the box. Your cousin stopped by here yesterday on his way to DC. I gave him the key to the box and paperwork to show the bank he had access to it. Though they should know that."

Stunned, she thanked her and hung up. She thought Franklin had gone to DC very early. He'd certainly left the house then. And he might not have lied about his day, but he'd certainly omitted something important. Did he have the deed now? Did he want to contest the will?

Feeling wounded, she went to the living room and turned on Uncle Benjamin's computer again. She'd looked at his family history material, but hadn't dug for any correspondence.

She rationalized that she'd been left the house and Uncle Benjamin had said she and Franklin could sort out what he wanted. She wanted the computer. Or at least what was on it.

The Documents folder had a lot of files and sub folders. Some contents were apparent — insurance, truck, landscape firm, historical society. Others were less obvious but made sense when you got in them — gravel dealt with the long drive that ran from the street. She opened a file called 'estimate' and found out what it would cost to go from gravel to asphalt. No way would she ever have that kind of money.

She went back to the C drive and did a search of all folders for the name Clara. Dozens of files appeared, including one titled Clara Baby that he had essentially hidden in the folder that held scans of long-ago tax files.

One document, titled only "Digger," stunned her.

Dear Digger,

I know you'll find this if I kick the bucket before we talk about it. I have been told that Aunt Clara may have had a baby before we married. I'm not sure who the father was, and if she did have a child, she gave it up for adoption.

I probably will never learn more than I know now. My great sadness is that she never told me. I guess the baby was gone years before we met, but I would have loved that little one like my own.

At this point, my big concern is that someone might try to fleece Franklin. They could say that any money I leave him was the product of Clara's and my marriage, making it at least in part to be claimed by an heir of hers. I don't know how all that works legally, and I certainly have no objection to helping someone.

Please don't look into this. It may not even be true. All I have is a handwritten note and a letter from a lawyer. Either one could be as made up as a fairy tale. When the lawyer asked, I declined to meet a supposed adult child. Why would a child who could prove the relationship hide behind a lawyer for something so important?

I had urged Franklin to take a DNA test, just for fun, but now I'm glad he didn't. Maybe someday he will and will learn he has a half-sibling somewhere.

I debated talking to Eunice about a baby, but I haven't talked to the old buzzard since the time she cussed me out for giving her copies of pictures of her and Clara and their parents. She wanted the originals. That was a year or two after Clara died.

Why am I telling you this instead of Franklin? I plan to talk to him, but I'll have to pick my time. If I'm too chicken and someone shows up after I die, let him know it could be for real. That'll get him to take the damn DNA test. UB

Digger's eyes stung. Aloud, she said, "Loved that little one like my own."

She supposed he meant to print and sign it. Maybe she'd find a signed copy somewhere. Better yet, a note addressed to Franklin.

Digger blew her nose. She was tired of crying, tired of moping around, feeling directionless. She would go to Frostburg and pick up the photos she'd had printed. She might have to go again tomorrow, but the trip would make her feel better.

She splashed water on her face and decided to wear make-up so she didn't look like a zombie. On the way out of the house, she put out food for Bitsy and Ragdoll. On second thought, she placed Ragdoll's on the kitchen table to keep Bitsy from eating it.

THE DRIVE FROM MAPLE Grove lifted Digger's spirits. From the interstate she could look over the edge of the mountains and see valleys coming to life after winter snows.

Every time she drove on the highway it was a reminder of how rugged the Maryland mountains were. Engineers plowed through peaks thousands of feet high so people could get from one town to another easily. The massive rocks on either side of the highway gave a sense of how challenging that must have been

If she could think of everyday things like that, distract herself from the deep sorrow of Uncle Benjamin's murder, she would get through the next few days.

As she neared Frostburg, Digger saw the sign for Midlothian. That didn't help her forget about Uncle Benjamin. She averted her eyes and continued to Frostburg, arriving at four o'clock.

She picked up the photos first, then drove to the university. She'd graduated from Frostburg State six years ago and had a strong sense of melancholy as she drove toward the campus.

She parked near the library and sat on a bench to watch students run to what would probably be the last class of the day.

She didn't feel old, but seeing students in shorts and sweaters in the cool weather reminded her of the sense of invincibility she'd felt at that age.

She liked her job and her town, but really, what had she done with her life? By now she had planned to write a history of skiing in Western Maryland, or maybe how living in a rural community affected career choices. Something interesting if not lofty, anyway. Instead she'd dated Damion and became distant from some of her friends. She'd realized only later that they didn't want to be around him.

She shoved those thoughts aside. She had come to Frostburg to take her mind off sad things. She stood and began to walk briskly through the campus.

WHEN DIGGER GOT BACK to the Ancestral Sanctuary at six-thirty, she had dozens of photos, two large bulletin boards she'd gotten at the office supply store, and an empty bag of M and Ms.

Bitsy greeted her with a long whine, unusual for him, and incessant tail-wagging. She let him into the front yard, knowing he'd come back because he was hungry.

Also greeting her was the smell of fresh air. She peered through the house. Curtains that hung over the back door's glass panes blew slightly.

She stood still for half a minute. If someone had been in the house, they seemed to have left. She turned on the hall light, as well as the dining room and kitchen lights as she walked.

Sure enough, the window by the back porch showed signs of force, but the nails she had placed in the frame had prevented opening from the outside. The glass in the door was a different matter. Someone had broken one pane and reached in to unlock the door.

She stood in the kitchen, listening to the quiet. Should she call the sheriff? Probably.

In a minute, Bitsy yelped to come in and immediately walked to his bowl. Digger poured dry dog food into it and remembered she hadn't seen Ragdoll. While the cat had recently hung out with Bitsy, she usually stayed aloof. But even so, it had been hours. Ragdoll's food sat untouched on the kitchen table. "Damn. Where is she?"

Though she thought she was alone in the house, Digger decided not to go upstairs. She did a methodical search for Ragdoll on the first floor. When she got to the half-bath, she frowned. The hand towel sat crooked on its rack. She didn't remember leaving it that way, but perhaps Franklin had two days ago and she hadn't noticed.

Digger eventually realized she would have to check the cellar, if only to see if the litter box had been used. Since Ragdoll used the pet flap in the door to get down there, she wouldn't have had to meow to get to her box.

Digger trod slowly and quietly down the cellar steps. *You can't find anything worse than the last time.*

And she didn't. Throughout were the same shelves — carefully organized — a large workbench, tools on pegboards, and garden equipment. A snow shovel and long broom that usually stood next to some shelves were against the wall. Probably to allow room for the gurney. "Ugh."

No sign of the cat. Digger walked to the laundry basket that had caught the sheets she'd placed in the chute on the second floor. She wouldn't have to get Franklin to escort her down here for that. She'd have to thank Ragdoll. She started the washer and returned to the kitchen.

She almost expected to see Ragdoll calmly eating her food, pleased to have a hiding place Digger couldn't discover. Now she was really worried. How would she explain to Franklin that she'd lost Uncle Benjamin's cat?

She called from dark front porch. Ragdoll rarely snuck out. Would she be able to find her way home in the dark? "Of course she can, she's a cat."

Back in the kitchen, Digger thought she heard a faint yowl from outside. She stood on the back porch, and Bitsy joined her. "Ragdoll?"

This time a clear meow came from the direction of the graves. "You have got to be kidding me. The graveyard at night?"

Digger went back inside and grabbed a flashlight from under the sink. "Come on, Bitsy."

The half-moon didn't offer much light, but at least the stars shone through the few clouds. She shivered in the fifty-degree darkness. She shone the light around the edge of the house, then toward the two large garden plots. No way would she be lucky enough to find her there.

Digger trudged up the incline and shone the beam around the graves closest to her. The meow came again, this time from the center of the little cemetery. Branches crunched from her right and she whirled.

Nothing moved. "Raccoon, has to be. Could be deer." *Don't be so jumpy*. Anyone trying to poach deer wouldn't get this close to a house.

Bitsy bounded ahead of her and sat next to the plywood that covered the grave, now ready for Uncle Benjamin. She barked, and a corresponding meow came from inside the grave.

"Good God." Digger hurried to the spot. Phelps and his partner had placed three cinder blocks atop the plywood, so she lugged them to one side. The huge piece of plywood was awkward to move, so she bent over and slid it a couple feet to one side.

Two yellow eyes stared up at her. Ragdoll growled, then meowed.

Digger grabbed Bitsy's collar. "You aren't going in there. Even if you got in, you'd break a leg. Sit." Bitsy half muttered and half whined.

The tarp that covered the dirt had long two-by-fours placed around the bottom. Digger placed her flashlight on the ground and grabbed one. She stuck it into the hole and peered in. "Come on, cat, you can walk up that." Ragdoll seemed to disagree, so Digger angled it more, making for a less steep climb.

Tail arched, Ragdoll walked up the wood, sniffed Bitsy, and ran toward the house. Bitsy followed.

"You're welcome." Digger replaced the plywood and two-by-four. "How in the world did she get down there?" Surely the cat would have protested if the two cemetery employees had placed plywood over her exit. Had they put her down there? Wait, Digger didn't remember letting her out of the house.

The grass was damp and she half-slid down it en route to the house. She was tempted to find Phelps' home phone number and ask him if he'd ever left a kid in a grave.

She let the animals into the house and stomped on the mat at the back door to get loose grass and twigs off the bottom of her shoes. How had Ragdoll gotten outside? Digger wasn't used to a cat, so it was possible Ragdoll snuck out as she was going in and out.

The crooked hand towel came to mind. And the door to Uncle Benjamin's closet, with Aunt Clara's jewelry box. Digger had no idea how many people besides her and Franklin had keys. She couldn't blame him for not changing the locks. It was her job now.

Her ringing cell phone interrupted her thoughts. Franklin's name popped up on Caller ID. "Hey cuz, will I see you soon?"

She hoped so. She started to tell him about Ragdoll and that someone had been in the house, but what would that accomplish? He'd be worried about her, and he couldn't do anything about the situation until he got there.

"Uh. No. How selfish will you think I am for staying one more night? Some friends from work have met Dad, and they wanted to take me to dinner."

Her stomach clenched. She wanted company in the big house! "Not selfish at all. There isn't much to do here. Probably calls tomorrow after the obituary's in the paper."

"Right. Some people have my cell. You can let others go to the answering machine."

Digger smiled to herself. She doubted she'd be able to find a replacement tape. "It'll be good to talk to people. Oh, did Sheriff Montgomery get you?"

"Yeah. Not much progress, but it's early."

"He won't let go of it. Take some time with friends. It'll be a sad weekend." Digger hung up.

Tomorrow she would buy a piece of glass and some glazing compound at the hardware store. For now, she retrieved an empty file folder from Uncle Benjamin's desk and used masking tape to secure it to the back door.

Someone could return, though she doubted it. Before she walked through the house to see if anything was missing, she tilted one of the metal kitchen chairs under the doorknob and piled it with pots and pans. She'd hear an intruder.

If she knew how to affix a pot of water above the door, she would. Perhaps a skill to learn.

She inspected the other windows on the first floor. They were almost four feet off the ground. They remained locked and the nails had not been disturbed.

Her foot was on the bottom step heading upstairs when she realized that someone could be up there. Not likely, but a possibility. As she looked up the staircase, Bitsy and Ragdoll romped down, eager for attention.

"You guys would bark if anyone was up there, right?" She jogged up the steps.

Every room showed some signs of having been searched, though the potential (or fulfilled?) burglar probably thought they had covered their tracks.

The bed's dust ruffle in Digger's room was crooked and a drawer in the chest had not been shut all the way. In Uncle Benjamin's room, the rocking chair stood a couple feet farther from the window and a few pieces of remaining clothes in the closet hung awkwardly on their hangers. Someone must have checked all the pockets.

She took her cell phone from her pocket and made the Ancestral Sanctuary's second call in three days to the sheriff.

CHAPTER TWENTY-TWO

DIGGER WOKE EARLY ON FRIDAY, before the weekly *Maple Grove News* hit the front porch. She dressed quickly and carried her laptop downstairs so she could check her email while coffee brewed. After less than five hours of sleep, she needed caffeine.

Deputy Jim Sovern hadn't stayed long the prior evening. He wanted a list of anything missing, but she couldn't give him one. When he dusted the front of the dresser in each room, he said it was clear the intruder had worn gloves. He liked the idea of the chair with pots and pans, and said he'd have the car on patrol drive by a couple of times overnight. He said he'd file a report and Digger should order at least a doorbell camera.

She fed the animals almost absently as she brewed coffee and made toast. While she drank her coffee and ate, Digger pondered the break-in. News of Uncle Benjamin's death was all over town, so a potential burglar could think no one would be in the house. Had he told friends about his Y2K cash, and someone casually mentioned it to someone not so friendly? A burglar looking for cash might not bother with a laptop, but why not Aunt Clara's jewelry box?

Or perhaps she interrupted someone when she drove up last night. She didn't like that idea. She used her phone to order two doorbell cameras from Amazon. Delivery not until Monday, but Franklin would be home between now and then.

Ragdoll leapt onto the kitchen table and Digger stroked her head. "You're getting some really bad habits. She lifted the protesting cat to the floor. "Who put you in that grave last night? They should be easy to spot. I bet you scratched the daylights out of them."

She went back to her phone and turned to the newspaper's front page, which was the only portion of it online. The lead story was Hofstedder's article on Uncle Benjamin's murder.

The story didn't provide anything new except that the ME had narrowed the likely time of death to between four-thirty and seven PM on Monday. Digger winced. If she had shut off the water at her house and driven straight to Uncle Benjamin's, she might have prevented his murder.

Or been killed, too.

She couldn't change the past in her own life any more than in American history. She needed to stop thinking about it.

As she stood to get a second cup of coffee, her cell phone rang.

"Digger, this is Abigail. We'd heard your uncle's death might not have been an accident, but it wasn't until we read the paper that I realized how certain the sheriff was."

Digger accepted the condolences and said she and Franklin didn't need anything.

"Mr. Stufflebeam would like to send flowers or make a donation."

Digger didn't need to think. "Either would be okay, but you know how he loved the historical society. I wish we'd put that in the obit."

Abigail finally hung up and Digger changed her outgoing message to let people know she was okay and that the Saturday service at the funeral home started at one. Another funeral was to take place in the morning. Initially Digger had not liked the late start. Now she was glad. Maybe she could sleep in a bit tomorrow.

Digger went to Craig's List and local Facebook Groups that sponsored online garage sales. Nothing she saw looked like any of Uncle Benjamin's possessions. No baseball cards, either.

She figured whoever went through the house was looking for cash. Uncle Benjamin had a lot of books, good furniture, and a few collectibles, but unless someone sold them in another state, items could be identified.

He generally shopped with cash, so people would assume he kept some in the house. They wouldn't have to know about his

Y2K stash. Where would he hide money? She tried to think as he might have.

He could've stuck bills in books, but it would have taken a lot of them, and someone might have picked up one to read. Heck, she would periodically borrow some of his local history books.

Under loose floorboards? Maybe drawers of his desk had hollow sections under what appeared to be drawer bottoms. She looked. Nothing. She and Franklin would have to decide if they really wanted to conduct a methodical search for either cash or ideas of what might be missing.

At ten o'clock a car came up the driveway. Digger glanced out the front window and wondered why a florist would bring flowers to the house rather than the funeral home. When she saw the huge bouquet of tulips, she realized it was for the reception at the house.

She accepted the vase from the delivery guy, an awkward-acting man of perhaps twenty. "Thanks for driving all the way out here."

"Sixty degrees, are you kidding? It's great to be outside." He shifted his feet. "I met him. He talked to every high school history class about how Garrett County was settled."

"I didn't realize he did all of them."

"Yep. I'm sorry he got killed."

Digger tried to be gracious, but she found his bluntness disconcerting. As he drove away, she decided it would be good practice for tomorrow.

The card was signed by "Benjamin's Historical Society Friends." She placed the flowers on the dining room table and delighted in how they brightened the room. She walked through the first floor opening the shades at all the windows.

Enough melancholy! She decided to spend a couple of hours looking through the house. She didn't expect to find any money or crown jewels, but it would also help her to know what Uncle Benjamin had. She knew her way around his kitchen, desk, the guest room, and bath, but hadn't explored every nook and corner. Why would she?

TWO HOURS LATER, DIGGER was stiff from bending, stretching, and climbing as she searched the house. She found no cash or anything exciting, though she now knew where Uncle Benjamin had hidden two diaries, one his own and one that appeared to have belonged to his father. She left them in the back of the hallway linen closet and made a mental note to tell Franklin about them.

She decided to fix lunch. After she ate, she would go back to Frostburg to get the rest of the photos she'd had developed at Walgreens.

She changed to more presentable clothes — including a button that asked "Have You Hugged a Genealogist Today? -- and selected a Mozart CD from Uncle Benjamin's basket of music.

Before getting on the Interstate, she stopped at her house to check on Jackrabbit's progress fixing the holes in her walls. She sat in front of her bungalow for almost two minutes. She'd been so happy to move out of apartments into the house, and now she would probably sell it. She couldn't justify two homes, even though the Ancestral Sanctuary didn't have a mortgage.

She did wonder if winters would be lonely. Weather in the mountains was very different from the rest of Maryland. One time when going to DC, she and Uncle Benjamin had driven through steady snow for an hour, but found none as they approached Hagerstown, Maryland. Just a breeze and cold temperatures.

Jackrabbit's car sat in her driveway, but the house was locked. Digger used her key and called to him as she entered. The sound of a sander floated down from the upstairs bathroom. No wonder he couldn't hear her.

When the sander stopped, she called up from the base of the stairs. "You busy up there?"

Jackrabbit appeared at the top of the steps, half-covered in drywall dust. "Hey Digger." He smiled as he removed his painter's hat, revealing his well-known ears.

"Thought I'd pop in to see if you needed anything. Tomorrow Franklin and I will be busy with the funeral all day."

"Yeah, that'll be awful. Sorry about your uncle."

"Thanks. How's the wall repair going?"

"You can come up, but it's kind of messy up here. I taped the wallboard and I'm sanding. I'll let it sit overnight and clean up and paint some tomorrow."

"Will you be able to repair the kitchen ceiling?" Digger crossed her fingers behind her back. She didn't want to have to hunt for a contractor.

"Yep, but not 'til next week. "I got a job to paint the kitchen at the fire station tomorrow."

"Sounds like fun."

He shrugged. "It's okay unless their siren goes off. They must all be deaf."

"You need more money yet?"

"Nope. I got an account at the hardware store, so they'll bill me and I'll bill you. Cameron gave me a check from you. It should cover most of my time."

"I'm heading over to Frostburg to pick up a few things. You have my cell, I think."

"Yep." He put his hat back on. "Hope tomorrow goes okay."

Digger headed to the kitchen and peered at the large hole in the ceiling. She could kill Damion.

Jackrabbit's sander started again, so she headed out before the sound became a permanent buzzing in her ears. She couldn't imagine that he wasn't half deaf.

The air smelled fresh so Digger lowered her car windows as she left town. I-68 was more crowded than yesterday. Probably people going away for the weekend or heading to DC to sightsee.

As she neared Frostburg, she again paid attention to the exit for Midlothian. She had driven by it hundreds of times of course, but she hadn't known Anna Jean Burke then. The woman had said she was going to stay in Maple Grove for a couple of days, so she might not be there.

Two days in a row. The temptation was too great. Maybe Digger could drive into town and figure out where Anna Jean lived. Heck, she could look it up on her phone.

She took the exit and drove slowly down the ramp. The part of the small town closest to the highway had few houses, and one was smaller than the others. She remembered Sheriff Montgomery saying Anna Jean's was a small one near the interstate.

Digger drove toward the post office and parked near it. She took out her phone, put in Anna Jean's name, and got the address.

A knock on her car window brought her up short. She pushed it down and smiled.

A woman asked, "Are you lost Dearie?"

"Just checking an address."

"Okay, I knew you weren't from around here. Do you need help finding something?"

Digger shook her head. "No, thanks. I'm all set."

That didn't seem to be the answer the woman expected, because she frowned and moved away.

Great, she'll remember me the next time someone asks her if she's seen anything suspicious.

Digger turned her Jeep around and drove back toward the interstate. Sure enough, the smallest of the three houses matched the address she had looked up. The neatly kept brick house had a small flower garden on each side of the front walk. Leading to the front door was a steep flight of stairs, typical of house on steep hillsides.

Anna Jean's car was not in sight, and the only garage was an old frame one behind the house. Its door stood open. Digger wasn't sure why she had wanted to look at the house. Somehow it made Anna Jean seem more like a real person than a caricature.

Had Uncle Benjamin been to this house? Maybe he had even spent the night here. Though he usually let her know if he was going out of town, there would have been no reason to mention a short stay over at the home of a foxy lady. Digger sighed. He didn't usually date such colorful women. But if he'd had a good time, more power to him.

She took her car out of park and was about to drive on to Frostburg when Anna Jean's red Buick barreled down the road and turned into the driveway. Digger's was the only car parked in front of her house. She would be spotted. Better to take the upper hand.

As Anna Jean parked near the steps, Digger opened her car door, shut it, and stood by her car. The sound of the door shutting drew Anna Jean's attention. She glanced at Digger and then gaped.

Digger raised one hand and waved with her fingers. After fully three seconds, Anna Jean found her voice. "Digger! I didn't expect to see you here. Come on in."

And I didn't expect to see you. Digger walked across the road and up the driveway to the base of the steps. By this time Anna Jean was at the front door, unlocking it.

Anna Jean let herself in and Digger heard the sounds of someone hastily tidying up. She recognized the drill. When she got to the door, sure enough Anna Jean was piling some newspapers under a lamp table, and hastily picking up a few scattered items of clothing and depositing them on one chair.

The house was a good size for one person, but very different than being in Uncle Benjamin's spacious home. Carpeted floors rather than hardwood, low ceilings, and small rooms. As she stood in the entry of the small Cape Cod house, Digger took in the dining room ahead of her and a short hallway to the left of the living room, which probably led to the bedrooms.

She couldn't put a name to the decorating scheme. If she had to, it would be midwestern traditional with a side of mauve.

Anna Jean finished her quick tidy and gestured to a rocking chair. "Have a seat Digger. I'm so glad you came by."

Digger sensed that wasn't true, but she preferred a welcome rather than a "what in the heck are you doing here" question. "I'm driving to Frostburg to pick up some photos at Walgreens. When I saw the Midlothian sign, I thought you might be here, so I looked up your address and stopped by on a whim." That last part was actually true.

Anna Jean sat across from her on a mauve-colored, two-cushioned couch. "Pictures of Benny? Oh, I would love a couple. I have a few on my phone, but you probably know he wasn't big on having his picture taken."

Digger nodded. "He said that was for youngsters who had nothing better to do with their time than look at themselves and their friends." She smiled. "Probably true, but it's still fun to take them."

Anna Jean said nothing.

Digger's mind raced. She sat here in front of a woman she barely knew, but from whom she wanted some information. If she could only think about what to ask. "You mentioned that you met Uncle Benjamin at the historical society. What brought you over to Maple Grove, if you live here?"

"My family lived there for a couple of generations. My grandparents' names were Hawthorne and Donnelson."

Digger's eyebrows went up. "I went to school with Amanda Donnelson."

"Probably a distant cousin. My parents lived in Maple Grove when I was born, but moved to Oakland shortly afterwards."

Digger nodded. "Limited number of jobs in a town like Maple Grove."

Anna Jean shrugged. "My father tried different jobs and businesses. He never had Benny's success."

"I'm, uh, sorry to hear that. Did your parents know Uncle Benjamin and Aunt Clara?"

For the first time Anna Jean seemed uncomfortable. "Not that I know of. My parents or grandparents may well have met him there. But we never talked about that."

It hit Digger like a snow squall that, according to Sheriff Montgomery, Anna Jean was not the fifty-something she tried to pass herself off as in Maple Grove. Rather, she was the right age to be Aunt Clara's daughter.

That seemed preposterous. And Digger didn't know whether the baby had been a boy or girl. She couldn't ask if the woman had been adopted. Instead, she asked, "Did you go to college in Frostburg?" *Lame question.*

Anna Jean shook her head. "I worked for a while at various jobs. Then I took some computer spreadsheet and other courses. That made me more likely to be hired for jobs in accounting departments or something similar. I like working with numbers."

"I majored in history myself. People don't think it's practical, but you learn a lot about what has made people tick through the years."

Anna Jean stiffened. "Digger, I'm happy you stopped by, but this feels almost like an inquisition."

"I can see why you would say that. It's just been a shock to learn that Uncle Benjamin was so close to someone I'd never heard him talk about. I think you even used the word fiancée."

Anna Jean flushed. "I guess we never used that exact term, but we did talk about the future a lot."

"I get that." Digger pasted a cheerful smile on her face. "Did he show you the entire house?"

Anna Jean almost giggled. "Well, you packed that tote bag for me. I guess you saw I had some things strewn around the place."

Digger nodded. "We saw that a lot of Franklin's coin collection was spread out on the bed in his old room. I gather he was showing you some of that."

For the first time, Anna Jean frowned and stiffened. "It almost sounds as if you are asking me if I took down the coin collection."

Digger wanted to ask her how she knew it was up somewhere, as opposed to in boxes under the bed or something. Or how a silver dollar got in the pocket of her sweater. "I'm sorry. I didn't mean to imply that. He was just so neat all the time. I was surprised to see things out of place."

Anna Jean leaned back in her chair. "I guess we'll never know what he was doing that afternoon. Perhaps he was looking at the coins and was interrupted by something downstairs."

"He may have heard Ragdoll making a mess. I found a couple broken jars of things he had canned."

Anna Jean adopted what Digger thought of as a high school girl's flirty persona. "Oh he did love to can. I never met a man who liked it so much. I tasted his peaches, applesauce, and beans."

That was almost like a punch in the gut. Anna Jean must have spent substantial time in the house for Uncle Benjamin to have shared food he canned. He usually reserved it for family or gave some away as gifts.

"I didn't know Aunt Clara well. She died when I was quite young. I wish I had asked him more about her. You mentioned he took you out to the graves. Did he say much about her, or her growing up in Maple Grove?"

Anna Jean again looked flustered. "He talked about where she taught school, and how hard they worked to develop that hardware store into a thriving business. And of course he mentioned how happy they were when Franklin came along."

Digger grinned. "I may have heard a couple of those stories. I have a hunch Aunt Clara would have been glad to know he enjoyed himself." *Maybe not with you.*

Anna Jean smiled. "Why thank you, Digger."

"It's kind of funny that he dated someone almost thirty years younger than he was. He was old enough to be your father."

Anna Jean stood. "Digger, I have a lot to do. I plan to be at the service tomorrow at the funeral home, and will probably come out to the house."

Digger knew she had lost any opportunity to be chummy with Anna Jean. She felt she couldn't ask a direct question like "are you adopted?" She was the right age, but if she was Aunt Clara's daughter and slept with Uncle Benjamin, that would just be too creepy.

CHAPTER TWENTY-THREE

FROSTBURG'S SHOPPING AREA BUSTLED along as usual on a Friday afternoon. Digger first stopped at a hardware store to get a pane of glass and some glazing compound. She could have bought them in Maple Grove, but someone at the hardware store would want to know what had broken.

After her glass purchase, she wandered around Walgreens picking up things like plastic utensils for the meal after the funeral and dishwashing liquid. She talked to people and didn't feel as if she was in an artificial world defined by Uncle Benjamin's death.

At the photo counter, a familiar voice came from behind her. "Digger. I'm so happy to see you."

Holly was one of the few people Digger didn't mind running into.

"We were packing our desks when we heard about your Uncle Benjamin. Everyone was sorry you have to go through this."

"Thanks. I hadn't thought about my stuff. Do you think we've lost our jobs permanently, or it's just a furlough?"

Holly shook her head. "None of us really have an idea. There's talk that maybe the firm will be sold, but I can't imagine who would buy it."

"I ran into Damion on the street, and he said he still had his job."

Holly sat a bottle of Tylenol on the counter. "There's talk that he kept his job by saying bad things about a few of the rest of us. I can't believe Abigail or some of the others would believe him."

"You'd need to know where that story came from. It sounds like a rumor he would've started himself."

Holly laughed. "Probably so."

"What are you doing over here, anyway?"

"I was at the office supply store getting for a stand for my computer. I'm going to try to do some graphics work from home."

She looked beyond Digger and then back again. "I heard you're going to inherit your uncle's place. It's called the Ancestral Sanctuary, right?"

She nodded. "Franklin and I just found out. Kind of a shock initially. But Franklin seems okay with it."

Holly leaned closer. "I hear he's really rich now."

"I wish they didn't have to make the will public."

Holly looked over Digger's shoulder again. Digger turned her head. "See someone you know?"

Holly flushed. "No, I was debating whether to tell you something else."

Digger screwed up her nose for a minute. "If Damion tells people we're engaged, make sure to tell them it's the biggest falsehood you ever heard."

"No, that's not it. There was this older woman in the coffee shop in Maple Grove this morning. I think she said she was your uncle's sister."

Digger could feel herself reddening. "If it's who I think it is, she was... is, I guess, my Aunt Clara's sister, Eunice. She hasn't been around much, but when she heard Uncle Benjamin died, she came over from... I think the sheriff said Morgantown."

"I should maybe tell you some of the wild things she was saying."

Digger groaned. "I guess I'd rather hear it from you.

"She was talking about how he built his hardware business with her family's money. She thought when it sold she should have gotten some. Finally, the coffee shop owner came over and said your uncle was well liked and this Eunice should keep her opinions to herself."

"Good for him!"

"Well, then this woman, Eunice you called her, said there might be more family than anybody knew about."

Digger felt the color leave her face, and she leaned against the counter.

"My God, Digger, are you okay?"

Digger studied Holly's concerned expression. She forced herself to appear more relaxed than she felt. "Eunice was estranged from Uncle Benjamin, and even Franklin, as far as I can tell. And she must be in her eighties. I'm not sure she's operating on a full head of steam."

Holly smiled. "Hopefully, she won't make it hard for your cousin, or for you. I'd hate to see you in some big legal battle."

"I think I would hate it more."

Holly touched her arm. "Come on, Digger, I'm treating you to coffee and quiche at Starbucks. You look like you could use it."

LONG SHADOWS OF DUSK covered the road as Digger drove back to Maple Grove. She hadn't given any thought to where Eunice had housed herself. Morgantown wasn't too far away, but it was far enough that someone in her eighties probably didn't want to drive back and forth a lot.

What could Eunice possibly think she would gain by bad-mouthing Uncle Benjamin in a town where he had so many friends? Or maybe she just couldn't help being nasty.

It was the topic about more family that bothered Digger. Did she know what happened to that baby? If she did, would she try to get that person to go after part of Franklin's inheritance?

Digger didn't know how adoption laws worked in terms of a child's legal rights to a birth parent's assets. Surely a child adopted about 60 years ago or more would have no claim.

She really needed to talk to Franklin. But what would she say? I've known something for two days but didn't tell you? Wait, he wouldn't know when she found out anything. That was good.

She could say that she had found the computer files today and planned to show them to Franklin this evening. And in the back of her mind, she guessed that's what she had planned to do. Or maybe she had planned to put it off, but now she couldn't. Not with Eunice spewing foul ideas around town.

As Digger pulled into Maple Grove, her cell phone rang. Caller ID had Franklin's name. She'd half-wondered if he'd be at home when she arrived, but Mr. Check-Out-the-Bank-Box hadn't been in touch all day.

She pulled into the hardware store lot, thinking of the irony of where she would be sitting when she talked to Franklin.

His voice sounded tired. "I wanted to plow through and drive up there tonight. I'm planning to take a nap and leave about nine."

"So you should be here just after midnight. I didn't think you were going to work today."

"I hadn't planned on it. I'm sorry I haven't been there to help get ready for Dad's shindig. If it hadn't been in the paper, I'd push it back a few days."

"You sure you aren't too tired to drive? "

"Once I take a nap, I'll be good. I guess you'll be in bed before I get home. "

"I might be, but there's something we do need to talk about. You could wake me up. "

"If it's that important, tell me now "

Digger squared her shoulders. "I was going through your father's research files, the ones on top. I thought it would be a good distraction. You know how we work on that stuff together." She paused.

"And? "

"There were letters from a few months ago. From a lawyer saying that he thought your mom had a baby before she married your dad, and gave the child up for adoption."

Silence.

"The lawyer asked if Uncle Benjamin would be willing to meet the child, but he didn't say if it was a man or woman. There's no copy of what Uncle Benjamin sent back, but there's another letter from the lawyer saying he respected your dad's decision not to meet with whomever this is. "

"I can't believe he never talked to me about it. *I* might want to meet someone. "

"I can see that. I thought you should know, in case somebody showed up tomorrow. "

After about ten seconds, Franklin said, "This just gets worse. "

"Franklin, I'm really sorry about the house. "

"I have to admit, the more I think about it, the more irritated I am. "

Digger felt her stomach tighten.

"I don't blame you. I just wished Dad had talked to me about all of it."

"His lawyer said she thought he planned to when we all met in DC. Damn. Same day as his funeral, probably. Ugh."

Again silence. Finally Franklin said, "It's not your fault, and it's just a house. When it comes right down to it, I probably wouldn't have lived there."

"Thanks." But she didn't offer to have him become a co-owner, or out and out give it to him. She realized she wanted the Ancestral Sanctuary. Not just because she'd been close to Uncle Benjamin, but because it was part of her family's heritage in the Western Maryland mountains. She wanted it to stay that way.

Franklin blew out of breath. "And you never heard anything about his will leaving you the house? "

Didn't we just go over this? "Of course not. I would've insisted that he sit both of us down to talk about it. "

"I guess I believe you. "

Digger started to retort, but stopped. "I called Ms. Silver to see if she had the deed. She thought it was in the safe deposit box."

He gave a clipped response. "It was."

Franklin didn't seem willing to elaborate, so Digger changed the subject. "I just got back from Frostburg. You want me to wait to do the bulletin boards until you get home?"

"Bulletin…? Oh, sure. Maybe you could kind of organize the pictures and we could put them on the boards first thing tomorrow. Funeral's not 'til one."

There seemed to be nothing more to say, so they hung up.

Digger pulled out of the hardware store lot. Usually she was glad to see Franklin. Now she would dread the idea for a few hours.

CHAPTER TWENTY-FOUR

WEARY AS MUCH FROM sadness as shopping, Digger pulled into the circular driveway. She rested her head on the steering wheel for a few moments, then sat up. "You have pictures to organize, woman."

Because she'd ended up having coffee and quiche with Holly, she'd been gone for several hours. She'd left the porch light on, but still glanced around carefully and stood inside the hallway for a few moments.

No Bitsy and no Ragdoll.

"You've got to be kidding me."

Then she noticed two wrapped pound cakes sitting on the hallway bench, with a note saying, "For tomorrow. Thelma Zorn."

How many people have a key to this place? She'd get a locksmith on Monday.

She was amazed that Mrs. Zorn had let the animals out. She needed a flashlight and again grabbed the one from under the kitchen sink. She opened the door to the back porch. She couldn't see Bitsy, but she could hear him.

Digger sighed, but decided to grab a fleece jacket before going outside. Bitsy was probably happily romping in the woods.

She turned and passed the back stairwell that led to the second floor and then the door to the cellar. As she got past that, it opened abruptly. Before Digger could turn around, someone had punched her in the temple.

"What the...?" Someone else pushed her from behind and Digger had a fleeting image of a rose-colored, polyester pants suit as she pitched down the cellar steps.

WHEN DIGGER'S HEAD STOPPED spinning, she slowly pushed herself to a sitting position on the cellar floor. Her first thought was that she felt bruised all over. Her second was that she might die in the exact spot where Uncle Benjamin died.

Then she heard two women screaming at each other upstairs and thought she might have a chance to live through the evening. Eunice and Anna Jean?

Eunice's shrill voice carried downstairs easily. "If you hadn't left the mess in the pantry, I wouldn't have had to come over here to fix everything."

Anna Jean spoke at a bellow. "I had everything under control. If you hadn't pushed him down the steps, we would have been in the clear!"

"I didn't push him! I found him!"

Digger's brain didn't process anything more for at least thirty seconds. She thought the two women had met only briefly, after Uncle Benjamin died. Now it seemed they knew each other. How? And why would they be in the house together?

Digger's head pounded. Had they met at the historical society? No, Eunice didn't live in Maple Grove. If she'd been in town after a long absence, someone likely would have noted her and mentioned it to Uncle Benjamin.

Could Anna Jean possibly be Clara's daughter? Had Eunice always known who she was? Or could they have both done DNA tests and found each other recently?

Anna Jean's voice rose again. "That cash is here. He told me he took out $20,000 and he hardly spent any of it."

"I'm sure the tightwad was proud of it!"

But whether related or not, they weren't just working together to secure money for Anna Jean and family heirlooms for Eunice. They had each had a part in Uncle Benjamin's murder. If Digger didn't make it out of the cellar, would Sheriff Montgomery figure it out?

Digger reached into her pants pocket for her phone. Not there. Had she left it upstairs? She had to let someone know where she was. She needed help, and wanted everyone to know who killed Uncle Benjamin.

She crawled several feet to the bottom of the steps and used the railing to pull herself to her feet. Her eyes swept the area around her. Where was her phone? Had she left it on the kitchen counter?

Her one advantage was Digger knew every inch of this cellar. She was too big to hide in some of her childhood spots, but the cellar was huge, the same size as each floor above it.

To be certain Anna Jean and Eunice had a hard time searching for her, the first thing Digger had to do was unscrew the two light bulbs. Except she wasn't tall enough.

The yelling had continued unabated, but it seemed the women had moved from the kitchen to the living room. That meant they wouldn't be as likely to hear Digger if she made noise.

She mentally probed the cellar. The only things to stand on were the sawhorses Uncle Benjamin had placed the shutters on when he repainted them every five years or so. Digger could also see him sanding wood for shelves for the historical society.

Despite the throbbing in her head, Digger went to the northwest corner of the cellar and tried to lift a sawhorse. Usually it would be no problem, but today it made her temples throb more and caused sparks to converge in her eyeballs. She must have a concussion. Still, it had to be done.

She decided to frog-walk it across the floor. More shifting than lifting, but still exhausting. When she finally placed a sawhorse under one of the lightbulbs, she realized she wouldn't be able to stand on it and stay balanced. She sat on the sawhorse and rested her forehead in her palms.

"Wait a minute, Dummy. You don't need to unscrew the bulb, you can break it with a broom handle." The filament would still be in the socket, but without the bulb to keep out oxygen, it would burn out. That might be the only thing she remembered from high school physics.

Still woozy, Digger went to the opposite corner and retrieved the mop she had intended to use to clean the kitchen the day she found Uncle Benjamin. She thought the glass in the bulb would be so lightweight that Anna Jean and Eunice wouldn't hear it shatter.

She stood under the bulb, which looked more like two bulbs, and took a swing. She missed twice, then connected and managed to back up before tiny shards of glass fell into her hair. She half-stumbled across the floor and swatted the second bulb. Then she stood still, adjusting to the dark.

Anna Jean and Eunice would have flashlights or their phones, but they would be flustered by the dark. Even so, they would find her, unless…

She moved to one of the four narrow windows. On her tiptoes, she could just reach it, and she pulled it halfway open. In her dazed condition, she couldn't balance on the other sawhorse and squeeze through the tight space, but she could make the two women think that's what she'd done. She dragged it the short distance to the window.

The voices upstairs had gone silent. Were they talking quietly, or had they decided to leave? The light squeak of the door that led from the upstairs to the cellar gave Digger an answer. She moved to the space under the stairs and slipped into it.

She didn't want to get into the old trunk under the stairs — no telling how long the air supply would last or if she could let herself out. But she could squeeze behind it and lie in a ball. As she settled herself, the door above opened more fully, and a clicking sound reached her.

In a stage whisper, Eunice asked, "Is the light out?"

Anna Jean responded in a loud staccato. "No, auntie dear, she probably unscrewed the bulbs."

"I didn't think she was that smart," Eunice said.

"Digger?" Anna Jean spoke in a coo. "I'm sorry about our little dust-up earlier. I was just surprised at your questions today. You know how much I loved Benny."

"No one called him that," Eunice hissed.

"Shu…She never minded, did you Digger?"

Digger wasn't sure if she wanted to laugh or cry. She stayed silent.

"What's that smell?" Eunice asked.

Anna Jean made a sniffing sound. "I don't smell anything."

Eunice's tone was almost triumphant. "Fresh air. There're windows down there. I told you we shouldn't leave her alone."

Anna Jean's rapid footsteps were accompanied by loud swearing. "Damn it, she's," Anna Jean tumbled over the sawhorse Digger had left under the light bulb. "Oof! That little bitch!"

It gave Digger great pleasure to imagine Anna Jean sprawled on the floor. She covered her mouth with her hand to stifle a laugh. But the effort of almost laughing made her head spin.

Eunice clomped down a couple of steps. "Are you all right?"

"I'm lying here in the dark with a sore knee and splinters of glass in my palms. Does that sound all right to you?"

"Not really. Do you see her?"

The sound of wood sliding on cement seemed to indicate that Anna Jean was trying to hang onto the sawhorse to stand up. "I don't see a damned thing. Wait a minute."

Eunice's voice carried down. "She seems pretty strong. I think if she were down there, she'd have tackled you."

Anna Jean swore again and Digger could see a small amount of light to her right. Anna Jean had turned on her phone's flashlight. It quickly swept the cellar.

"She's gone." Anna Jean spoke fast and breathlessly. "We have to get out of here." She started up the steps.

Eunice shrieked. "I'm not going without my mother's photo album and brooch!"

"I don't give a crap about your mother's photo album. Or her brooch. It wasn't in her jewelry box."

So she had been in that closet.

"We can't be found here." Anna Jean moved rapidly up the steps. "Get out of the way!"

"Don't talk to me like that! You wouldn't be here if I hadn't told you about Benjamin Browning."

"Stuff it." Anna Jean's voice grew faint as she strode rapidly toward the front door. "And stay the hell away from me, Aunt Eunice." She said the last two words as if they were an extreme insult.

Eunice babbled after her, but Digger figured Anna Jean would be halfway down the driveway before the older woman got to the front door. She stayed curled in her ball and tried to assess her situation.

Eunice might be unable to get down the steps easily, but she could realize Digger was still in the cellar and block the door. If Digger's head weren't spinning, she would run up the stairs and out the back door. Right now, she couldn't imagine climbing two steps. She closed her eyes and drew steadying breaths.

Upstairs, Eunice walked from the front of the house to the kitchen and back to the living room. Thudding noises reached Digger. It sounded as if Eunice was randomly moving furniture or pulling things off shelves. Did she think she'd find her brooch in a teapot?

The *Star Spangled Banner*, on low volume, came toward her from wherever her phone had landed. She cheered momentarily, then realized that she would have to be unreachable for hours, maybe overnight, before anyone would grow concerned. And what would happen if Franklin came home in a few hours and Eunice was in the house?

At least the ringing had given her a rough idea of where the phone was. She peered out from her hiding place and saw its screen flash and then go dark as the ringing stopped. The phone was under the lip of the bottom step. No wonder she hadn't seen it.

More thumping. Did the woman think Uncle Benjamin had hidden the infamous brooch behind books in the glass-covered shelves? Or maybe she believed Uncle Benjamin had hidden money in the house. Digger didn't care.

She started to crawl from under the steps, when she heard a lighter thump, but not from upstairs, from in the cellar, near the open window. Digger strained her ears. She sensed rather than saw movement, but she didn't want to peer around the trunk.

Something heavy landed on Digger's backside, and she grunted. Then a cold nose probed at her ear. She whispered, "Ragdoll! Did they put you outside?"

The cat walked down her shoulder and onto the floor. She sat so close to Digger's face that all she could see was cat fur.

"Move, girl." Ragdoll put her nose on Digger's. She stifled a sneeze and it felt as if the top of her head would explode. "Did you see Bitsy? Did she get away?"

The cat didn't answer. She settled into herself, seemingly ready for a nap. Digger started to push her aside so she could crawl out.

The front screen door banged shut, and rapid footsteps moved into the living room. Much too fast for Eunice.

Anna Jean's sharp tone carried. "She's got to still be here. Her car's in the driveway. If she got out, she'd have driven away."

Ragdoll hissed lightly.

"I'm going downstairs again."

Oh...crud.

Eunice screeched. "If she's down there, she isn't going anywhere. You stay here and help me find my album!"

Anna Jean kept moving toward the cellar steps. "Benny left her this house. She and my precious half-brother have to have money. I deserve some of it."

Anna Jean yanked open the cellar door.

Ragdoll shot out from under the cellar steps as Anna Jean ran down them. Digger tightened her curl. How could Anna Jean possibly think she would end up with money? Even if she found Uncle Benjamin's Y2K cash, she'd have to run away or go to jail.

"You're no pixie, Digger. You didn't crawl out that window. I'm through playing around. Come out from wherever you're hiding and talk to me."

Digger said nothing. A bead of sweat trickled down her face, near her eye.

Anna Jean began a methodical search of the cellar. Her phone's flashlight beam moved every which way as she muttered to herself. "Couldn't make it easy. Plenty to share."

As Digger knew it would, the beam eventually found its way to Digger's hiding place. Anna Jean's knees cracked as she squatted to peer under the steps.

"You have to be back there, Digger." In a more genial tone, she added, "You don't want to lie on that dusty, cold floor. Let's go upstairs and I'll help you soak in a hot tub. You must be sore after your tumble."

Digger said nothing.

"I see the sole of your shoe."

Digger curled her toes, which made her shoe shift slightly.

"There you go, come on…"

Ragdoll's howl was half loud hiss and half mad-cat-yowl.

From upstairs, Eunice yelled, "What is that?"

Anna Jean swore. "My hand! You bit me, you mangy feline!" Another thump. "Ow! My head." Anna Jean had banged her head on the overhang. She backed away from Digger's hiding spot.

Faster than she thought she could move, Digger pulled herself from behind the trunk. If she could get the phone, she could dial 9-1-1. She spotted it under the bottom step.

Anna Jean jumped around the cellar, cursing and squealing, paying no attention to Digger. She slid three feet, grabbed the phone, and — head pounding — slid behind the trunk again. She tried to focus. You didn't need to put in a phone's password to make an emergency call, but you did need decent vision to push 9-1-1.

Ragdoll shot herself under the steps like a furry torpedo.

Anna Jean had stopped moving around and bent at the waist to look toward the trunk. "That stupid cat! She's always hated me. I hope it scratches the daylights out of you! My hand is bleeding!"

Digger tried to focus on the phone. "What did you do with Bitsy?"

Anna Jean's tone became friendly again. "She's tied up in the yard. Come on out, Sugar. You know I wouldn't hurt you."

Digger managed to push the numbers and press send, the phone making its distinct dialing sounds as she did so.

Anna Jean raged, "You have a phone, you bitch! Give it…"

Ragdoll hissed, ears back, and backed toward Digger.

Digger's voice was weak. "Send people, cars…"

"What's the nature of your emergency?"

Anna Jean screamed, "Give me that damn phone, Digger!" She reached under the steps and pulled on Digger's foot.

"She wants to kill me. Hurry." The phone slipped from Digger's finger's, but she hadn't pushed the disconnect button. She hoped Anna Jean could hear the commotion in the dispatch center. Maybe it would make her leave.

Anna Jean was silent for several seconds. In an ominous tone, she said, "Give me the phone, Digger."

Digger's voice was husky. "You'll get those purple pants dirty if you crawl under here, Anna Jean."

A scuffing sound, then Ragdoll hissed again.

Anna Jean's tone became resigned. "All I wanted was… something, anything. I had nothing all my life because that woman gave me away."

"Why didn't you just ask?" Digger said.

"I did! He didn't want to meet me."

Digger wasn't sure what to say.

"So I thought I'd just meet him somewhere. I didn't think he'd be sweet on me, but I figured, why not?"

From the top of the steps, Eunice called, "I told you to tell him right away!"

Digger ignored her and spoke in little more than a whisper. "Anna Jean, you didn't have to hurt him."

"I didn't! I just needed a little extra money. When he saw me in Franklin's bedroom, with the coins. I told him who I was."

Digger's mind felt clearer. "He had no idea?"

"No. He was pretty much horrified." Her voice caught. "He kept saying, 'I slept with Clara's daughter. I slept with Clara's daughter.'"

"My God," Digger muttered. *Poor Uncle Benjamin.* "Is that why you pushed him down the steps?"

"That was Eunice."

A stomp on the steps came from above them. "I did not. I hated that old goat for taking my sister from me, but I'd never want to spend the rest of my life in prison for killing him." She came slowly down the steps.

Anna Jean's voice had a reedy quality. "Now, Eunice. You don't want to go to jail for killing anybody. Put that little ol' gun away."

A gun? Really? How can this get any worse?

"Digger," Eunice said, "that mutt of yours is in the back yard. I'll shoot him if you don't tell me where my mother's brooch is."

"I don't know! Just take your stupid pictures and go."

Anna Jean's voice was almost a sob. "Eunice, I think she called the cops."

"You're making that up."

"I'm not! We have to leave."

Digger raised herself on one elbow. "I want to know who killed Uncle Benjamin!"

Damion's voice floated down. "I did, but you have to promise not to tell."

CHAPTER TWENTY-FIVE

NO ONE SAID ANYTHING as Damion walked a couple steps more toward the cellar. Digger peered at him from a crevice under the steps. She kept hearing the words, "I did." Her head pounded, but even as it did, she began to feel more clear-headed.

"Mrs…Eunice, is it? Hand me that toy gun of yours."

Her voice rose. "Who are you?"

"A good friend of Beth's." He did a gimme gesture. "I want the toy gun."

Her voice shaking, Eunice said, "This is not a toy!"

"If you want people to believe that, you should blacken the little orange cap on the nozzle."

Anna Jean laughed, an edge of hysteria to it. "You brought a cap gun?"

"You didn't bring any," Eunice snapped.

Anna Jean seemed to study Damion intently, and Digger wondered why.

Damion raised his voice. "Beth dear, is that you under the steps? Come on out."

Did he mean to do it? Digger thought everything Damion did was meant to benefit him. Uncle Benjamin's death wouldn't affect him one way or another, so why bother? "I'm coming, but my head hurts."

"Poor baby. If you'd stayed with me, you wouldn't be in this position."

As she crawled out, Digger saw Damion walk toward Eunice and grab the gun. She backed up, her limp again pronounced. Was it an act or did she move more poorly when under stress?

"Turn on that light," Damion said.

"Your girlfriend broke the bulb," Anna Jean said. She added, "I've seen you before."

Digger tried to lean on the stair rail to stand. "He's not my boyfriend."

"You should be so lucky," Damion said. He did a half-bow to Anna Jean. "You did. You drove by me when you left this lovely house a few days ago."

Finally upright, Digger looked up at Damion and was shocked to see him holding not Eunice's toy but what appeared to be a real handgun. "Where did you get that thing?"

He shrugged. "You know me, always the best. Too bad I didn't keep that standard when I dated you."

She lifted her chin. "You weren't there. You didn't really kill him."

"Sadly, yes. I stopped by to enlist his help in regaining your affections. He told me to leave but the old guy didn't lock the front door. I let myself in after he walked back to the kitchen."

"I called from the driveway. Your car wasn't here." She wasn't sure why she was arguing with Damion. It didn't make sense. Nothing made sense.

"I wasn't sure you'd be happy to see me. I parked just over the rise." He gestured behind him, to the spot where the road rose higher than Uncle Benjamin's property. "I was walking down from there when the red Buick sped by me. Lucky she didn't hit me."

Anna Jean's voice sounded panicked. "I won't tell anyone I saw you."

"Why were you coming here?" Digger asked.

"See, I envisioned your dear uncle agreeing that you and I were perfect for each other. Then we'd be sitting in his kitchen drinking that awful tea he makes, waiting for you to come spend the night."

Digger's throat tightened. "He never did a thing to you!"

"I didn't *mean* to hurt him. When I found him in the kitchen, he was cursing about someone breaking his jar of canned peaches." Damion looked at the other two women. "Which one of you two beauties did that?"

Eunice said, "I most certainly didn't."

Damion glanced at Anna Jean. "I take it that's an unstated yes?"

Anna Jean folded her arms across her chest and shuddered. "I was trying to get him to talk to me. He wouldn't listen, so I grabbed his elbow and he dropped the peaches and some smelly red pickles."

"Beets. Did you tell him who you really were?" Digger asked.

"I told her not to!" Eunice trilled.

Anna Jean faced Eunice, her face contorted. "He said he didn't want to go out anymore. What was I supposed to do?"

Damion's gaze flicked to each of the women, then landed on Anna Jean. "Not that I care too much, but who are you, really?"

Anna Jean shifted her gaze to Digger. "Did you figure it out before tonight?"

"I wondered, but it seemed too weird."

Anna Jean straightened her shoulders. "I had a right to be taken care of. I'm her daughter!"

Damion's eyebrows went up. "Whose daughter?"

Digger kept her eyes on Anna Jean. "My Aunt Clara's daughter. Born before she met Uncle Benjamin." She shifted to Damion. "What did you do?"

"When I informed him that I was staying until you got here, he poked me in the chest. The only thing close by was that cream pitcher on the counter. I didn't think I hit him that hard."

The cream pitcher I couldn't find the next day. Digger felt lightheaded again, but she had to know. "How did he get in the cellar?"

"He had the door to the cellar open, and he kind of fell in that direction."

"That's at least five feet from the pantry." Digger said. "He would have fallen on his back in the hallway."

Damion smiled, tightly. "He did. He stood up. Was very lightweight, easy to push." He frowned. "The cat was more of a problem, but it was easy enough to stuff away."

Digger felt bile in her throat. She could only imagine the fear Uncle Benjamin felt in those seconds. And the pain. She almost choked out the words. "Why would you do that?"

In a tone as casual as if he'd been ordering from a menu, Damion said, "I figured you'd inherit a lot. I'd help you in your time of great pain, and voila. Everybody's happy. I even drove back into town. I thought I'd offer you a ride up here, so I could comfort you when you found him. But you'd already left."

"So you did follow me up here!"

"Yes, but then I decided I should wait a bit. Come by when there were flashing red lights or something." He frowned. "I guess the sheriff thought I was just some lovesick guy trailing his old girlfriend."

Digger's throat tightened. She started to say something, but Damion stiffened and glanced over his shoulder. "Where's your cousin?"

Digger calculated whether she should lie and couldn't think of how it would help. "Not here."

He gestured with his weapon. "We don't want any visitors. Come on, ladies. Upstairs and outside."

"I'm not going anywhere," Eunice said.

Damion pointed his gun above her head and fired once. Eunice jumped backwards into Anna Jean, who pushed her away.

Digger's head, already pounding, now had ringing ears. The acrid odor of gun powder turned her stomach. For a brief second, she hoped someone had heard the shot, but they were in the cellar, and the Gardiner's home was at least a quarter mile away. With a sinking feeling, she remembered they both wore hearing aids.

Eunice, no longer limping, started up the steps as Damion backed up in front of her. "That's a good old gal."

Anna Jean met Digger's eyes. "Can you walk?"

"I think so. Maybe go ahead of me."

From near the top of the staircase, Damion called, "No tricks, Beth."

"Like that little trick you pulled at my house, to make the pipes leak slowly?"

He grinned broadly. "You and your good friend Cameron figured that out, did you?"

Digger didn't respond. She held onto the railing. Now that she was on her feet and moving, she wasn't as woozy. But she didn't want Damion to know that. She gripped the railing hard, feigning more difficulty than she felt.

At the top of the steps, Damion pointed to the left, his right, with his gun.

"Where are we going?" Anna Jean asked.

"To get some fresh air. I need you three out of the house while I check out some things."

What things? What could he possibly want?

They trudged out the back door and down the porch steps, Eunice tottering on the uneven ground without her cane.

Digger glanced at the moon, not yet high in the sky, and only half-full. Even if the Gardiners happened to be in their attic looking toward the Ancestral Sanctuary, they wouldn't see anything.

"Head up that little rise to the gravesites," Damion said.

From where he was tied up near the picnic table, Bitsy whimpered, then barked steadily.

Damion turned toward him.

"Don't hurt Bitsy!" Digger yelled.

"Get him to shut up!"

Digger stopped walking and faced her dog from about twenty yards away. "Bitsy. Quiet. Now!"

Bitsy whimpered and jumped around, straining on his lead. But he stopped barking.

"He better stay quiet," Damion said. "Or I will pop him."

They walked, and Digger glanced sideways at Anna Jean. "Who, uh, adopted you?"

"Some high school friends of Clara's, though I didn't know they knew my birth mother."

"Was their name Mumsford?" Digger asked.

"She should have given you to me to raise," Eunice shrieked.

Anna Jean stopped walking and faced Digger. "How did you know that name?"

"This is a fascinating story, but keep moving!" Damion said.

"I didn't. I saw their high school yearbook. She went to the prom with him junior year."

"No," Anna Jean said, "not Gregory Mumsford. I found out about him when I did the DNA test. But he was already dead. His much older — and stricter—cousin, Carl Hawthorne. But my parents never said they knew my birth parents. DNA led me to my dear auntie."

Digger couldn't imagine how hard it must have been for Aunt Clara to give up her little girl. Or had she been relieved to find someone she knew to adopt her, so she could get on with her life? Or did she know who took her? Maybe she did it through an agency of some sort.

Eunice's tone was bitter. "They took you away from us! I did the DNA test in case you wanted to find me."

Anna Jean almost sneered at her. "My parents told me they left Maple Grove because they wanted to get away from some annoying people. Now I know who they meant."

Digger thought of the photo of a delighted Eunice holding the bundle that had to have been Anna Jean.

Eunice said nothing for several seconds. Then she asked, "What's that tarp covering?"

"The dirt for Benny's grave," Anna Jean said.

"I'm getting my shoes dirty," Eunice muttered.

"No one cares." Damion waved the gun at them. "So just shut up."

Digger looked right and left. If she hadn't picked up all the fallen branches there might have been some sort of weapon.

They reached the trellis that bore the Browning name, and Damion said, "Move to the open grave."

"You took the plywood off," Digger said.

"What are you going to do?" Anna Jean asked.

"Nothing bad. Just put you out of sight for a few minutes. But you have to hurry, ladies." He gestured to the open grave.

Digger turned to him. "Did you search the house and put Ragdoll down there yesterday?"

"Yep. I thought it would spook you. If she hadn't hissed at me so much, I'd have put her in the pantry again."

When no one moved, Damion grabbed Eunice by the elbow and roughly propelled her to the open grave and shoved her.

She fell face-first into the hole, with a loud humph.

Digger figured Eunice had the air knocked out of her, or she would be screaming. She might not have gotten hurt, since it wasn't a long fall and she was, to say the least, well padded. On the other hand, if her neck turned the wrong way…

Damion grinned at Digger and motioned again with his gun. "Okay, Beth. You need a shove?"

Digger said nothing. She moved to the edge of the grave and sat on the rim. Then she pushed herself into it, careful to avoid landing on Eunice. She ended up at the head of the face-down woman. "Wait a second while I get Eunice sitting up."

Above her, Damion said, "Not waiting."

Digger bent to Eunice, whose eyes were wide and mouth open in an O. "Come on Eunice. I'll push you to sit up." That entailed getting Eunice onto all fours, no easy task. Digger reasoned it was better than having to pull her if she'd landed on her back.

Above them, Anna Jean said, "I'm not going in that dirty hole."

"Come on, Eunice." Digger breathed as she pushed, and her head felt as if it was swelling.

Feet seemed to move around at the edge of the grave and Anna Jean said, "Ow. You broke it!"

Digger had just gotten Eunice to sit on her tailbone when Anna Jean landed hard, feet first. She held one hand on her other shoulder. "He hit me with the butt of that gun."

"Too bad he didn't shoot himself," Digger muttered.

"You don't need to aim to shoot fish in a barrel," Damion said.

"What do you think you're doing?" Digger yelled.

"I don't need people talking about what they saw," he said.

Anna Jean opened her mouth to scream, but then she yanked her head to one side. A bullet thumped into the wall of dirt behind her and tiny clods of it sprayed the three of them.

Digger couldn't believe he was shooting. Would anyone hear? Would they think it was someone poaching deer, or would they call the sheriff?

"Well, hell. This is harder than I thought." Damion peered over the edge, his wild eyes and delighted smile those of a madman. "Maybe I need to…"

A thud above them made Damion pull up. "What?"

The faint sound of a siren drifted in. Digger momentarily shut her eyes in relief. She'd left her phone on in the basement. Had the 9-1-1 people figured out where the call had come from?

Another thud. Damion moved away from the edge of the grave. "Who is that?

Bitsy began barking wildly.

"Stupid dog!" Something else thumped above them.

"Don't shoot him!" Digger yelled.

Bitsy's barks grew fainter. Had someone unchained him and gotten him to move away?

The faint siren grew closer, but Digger thought it could be at least a mile away as the crow flies, longer by road.

Eunice had finally caught her breath. "You get the hell away!"

Two shots rang out above them. Even from a smaller gun, the sound was too loud for Digger's sore head.

How many shots had that been? One in the basement, one aimed at Anna Jean in the grave, now two more. Were there six in the gun?

Damion ran away from them, but then began coming back. Short of breath, he said, "No witnesses."

"My God," Anna Jean said.

"He means us," Eunice said.

"Stand against the side, so he's above us, not across from us," Digger ordered. She realized he could shoot each of them in the top of the head. She lowered her voice to a whisper. "And move from side to side, as quickly as you can. He's a lousy shot."

Something landed in the grave with them. Digger squinted. One of the large landscape stones Uncle Benjamin had placed next to the path that led to the cemetery. That was what someone up there was throwing at Damion! She had a wild impulse to giggle. A few days ago she'd been designing advertising for these landscape rocks.

But stones were no match for a gun.

Damion fired again, but this time he was aiming at something above ground. "I see you now, damn you!"

Five shots.

Digger turned to Anna Jean. "Put your hands together so I can stand on them to get out!"

"I want to go first," Eunice trilled.

"Shut up!" Digger and Anna Jean said.

Damion's yelling grew more faint.

Anna Jean bent over and leaned against the wall as she threaded her fingers. "Be careful."

Digger stepped on her fingers with her right foot, raised herself, and clawed to reach the top edge of the grave.

"Hurry, Digger. This is killing my shoulder."

Digger put her other knee into the wall to take some of the weight off her right foot. "Trying." She placed her cheek against the wall to help balance herself and was rewarded with lips coated in dirt.

Finally she had purchase and began slowly pulling herself up. In a few moments, her eyes could see over the edge of the grave. Damion was at least 100 yards away, his back to her, waving his gun as he tried to run over the uneven ground. Someone seemed to be ahead of him, but she couldn't tell who it was.

She kept pulling herself up and finally could bend enough to lie part of her torso on the ground. Anna Jean removed her hands and Digger wiggled and grabbed clumps of weeds until she lay, panting, on the ground.

"Now us!" Eunice yelled.

"Quiet," Digger hissed. "I have to stop him. I'll be back."

She spit dirt from her mouth and grabbed one of the oval stones that had landed nearby. She guessed it to be about six inches long. She bent at the waist and moved a few yards to kneel behind the headstone of her Great Grandfather Browning. She peered around it and was horrified to see Damion trudging back toward her.

She stayed crouched, prepared to move as he got closer, so she'd be on the other side of the stone as he approached.

As he neared them, she could make out his muttering. "Not worth this, not at all. But gotta get rid of the broads."

Broads? Who says broads? Digger gripped the landscape stone. She was tired and still dizzy. No way would she have the strength to hit Damion hard enough on the head to knock him out, or even down. But maybe, just maybe, she could knock the gun out of his hand.

She felt thankful it wasn't summer. The soggy spring ground would keep him from hearing her move around.

Damion stopped. He looked behind him. "Run away, you coward!"

Digger pulled her legs closer and ducked her head. She wouldn't be able to see him if he started in her direction. She held her breath.

Damion walked past her, just ten feet away. When he was a few feet beyond, she peered over the top of the headstone. His back was to her.

She leapt out, raised the stone, and brought it down hard on the back of his right hand.

The gun fired as he let go of it. Had he had his hand on the trigger? She shoved his back with her shoulder, but he stayed rooted to the spot.

Damion turned his head. "Beth, how in the hell did…" He half turned and pushed her with his now-free hand.

As she started to fall backwards, Digger had the presence of mind to crook her elbow and put her arm behind her head. With a sense of slow motion, she watched Damion start to bend over to pick up his gun.

A blur of black and brown fur torpedoed past and hit Damion in the shoulder, knocking him to his knees.

"Bitsy! Don't hurt my dog!"

Her rear end landed on the ground and her head, protected by her arm, followed with a small bounce.

From the grave, Anna Jean screamed. Digger had a second to see the irony in that before another person stumbled past her and into Damion, knocking him onto his stomach.

"Stay down you bastard!"

The voice sounded familiar, but Digger still saw stars of her own making, so she didn't sit up. "Bitsy, come here."

Panting, the dog lay next to her and put both paws on her chest. Then he began methodically licking the dirt from her face.

CHAPTER TWENTY-SIX

DIGGER KEPT A HAND ON Bitsy's head as she watched Marty Hofstedder kneel on the small of Damion's back. He placed a hand on Damion's shoulder so he couldn't try to sit up. "I said stay down!"

"What are you doing here?" Digger asked.

He glanced at her. "Brought a picture of a colonial pitcher from an antique shop in Frostburg, to see if it was your grandfather's. I can go if you like."

She half-smiled. "You can stay." She sat up, slowly.

Now there was not only the sound of sirens but of a V-8 engine roaring up the driveway. Digger looked at the no-longer squirming Damion. "Great job, Hofstedder."

"Digger?" Anna Jean had adopted a plaintive tone. "Can you get us out of here, Sugar?"

Though a sheriff deputy could catch her, she didn't want Anna Jean running into the woods, so she used a delay tactic. "I'll get the ladder from the shed and lower it to you."

"I'm sure you could pull me up."

"Me first," Eunice said.

"Shut...be quiet, Eunice," Anna Jean said.

Digger smiled at Hofstedder. "Anna Jean, I'm sorry, my head is pounding. I just bumped it again. No way could I pull you up."

"Kneel down and let me stand on your back," Eunice said.

"Shut up, Eunice," Anna Jean said.

Bitsy went to the edge of the grave and barked twice.

Car doors slammed in the front of the house. A man's voice called her name. Digger sat up, but she didn't think her head would like her shouting.

"Back here," Hofstedder called. "In the graveyard!" He nodded toward Digger. "Anything I should tell them after you pass out?"

"I'm not going to pass out."

"Put your head on your knees," he said.

She did, which brought some uprooted daffodils into her line of sight. They must have been moved, but clumsily, when the men dug Uncle Benjamin's grave. She'd have to replant them. *Why are you thinking about daffodils?*

Hofstedder said, "Your color's getting better. That deputy, Charlie, and one I don't know are running toward us."

"Beth." Damion's voice was hoarse. "You know I'd never hurt you. Tell him to let me up so I can explain how I was helping you."

Digger raised her head. "You didn't have to kill Uncle Benjamin. He didn't do what you wanted so you decided to hurt him. What you always do."

"Jesus," Hofstedder pushed Damion's shoulder harder. "Who kills an old man?"

CHARLIE MCBRIDE AND JIM SOVERN subdued Damion with little problem, but a great deal of protest.

"Beth asked me to help her!"

"Shut up, Horner," Charlie said.

"Who's Beth?" Jim asked.

The two men hoisted Damion to his feet. They pulled his arms behind his back and handcuffed him.

Charlie spoke to Jim. "Put him in the back of your car, and call for a couple ambulances, would you?"

"Will do." He propelled Damion down the small hill and along the side of the house.

"Let us out of here!" Eunice yelled.

"Please," Anna Jean added.

"Just a sec. Gotta make sure Digger's not hurt too bad." He walked the few steps to where Hofstedder and Digger sat with their backs against a headstone, and squatted in front of them. "You don't look so hot."

"I got shoved down the cellar steps."

Charlie's eyes widened. "I'm glad it ended up different for you."

Digger winced.

"Tactful," Hofstedder said.

"Sorry. So, Digger, I want the EMTs to check you out. Sit here, don't walk around before they get here."

The fall to the ground hadn't really hurt Digger, but she felt less steady on her feet. Or thought she would. "Fine by me."

Charlie walked the short distance to Uncle Benjamin's open grave and began explaining why he wanted to wait until the EMTs arrived to help them out.

Digger turned to Hofstedder. "Are you the one who called earlier?"

"Yeah. I wanted to swing by with the pitcher. Took a chance you or your cousin would be here and drove on out."

She glanced around the headstones, happy not to be soon among them. "Good timing."

Hofstedder nodded to Charlie's back. "Who are those two women?"

"It's a long story."

"From a reporter's perspective, that's the best kind."

CHAPTER TWENTY-SEVEN

FOUR HOURS LATER, after a brief visit to the urgent care office in town, Digger sat in the Ancestral Sanctuary kitchen — her kitchen — across from Marty Hofstedder and Franklin. She would rather have been alone, but she owed her life to Hofstedder and an explanation to her cousin.

Hofstedder had a piece of paper in front of him, with scribbled notes. "Digger, do you have a computer I can use to file a story?"

"My laptop's on the bed in the first guest bedroom upstairs. You can use it and when you're done, I'll show you how to get on Wi-Fi."

In silence, Digger and Franklin listened to him jog up the steps.

Franklin stood and poured himself a second cup of coffee. "I'm sorry I was angry with you about the house."

"I'm sorry I didn't tell you when I first found the lawyer's letter about your mom."

He sat at the table again. "When were you sure it was Anna Jean Burke?"

"When they both showed up, tonight. They were here, briefly, yesterday, but they didn't come together or act as if they knew each other. Even then, it was only a weird guess until I heard her call Eunice 'auntie.'"

"When was that?"

"After I landed on the cellar floor."

Franklin held Digger's gaze. "I'm glad you weren't killed, cuz."

Digger smiled briefly. "Me, too."

Franklin shook his head. "You sure she actually dated Dad?"

"Mr. O'Bannon thought so, and you saw she had stuff here."

"Oh, right. I just don't get it. If she'd showed up and said who she was, I think Dad and I would have been glad to meet her. After we got over the initial shock and checked her out, I guess."

"I would have, if she'd have cut out the perfume."

Franklin sat up straighter. "Wait. How did she find Dad?"

"She did an Ancestry DNA test and found Eunice. I think at first she might have been simply trying to find her biological family."

"And then she figured out Dad had money?"

Digger rubbed her neck. "There's a lot more to find out, but when Eunice was here the first time, she talked about how Uncle Benjamin got some of the money for the hardware store when Aunt Clara took her retirement money out, when she stopped teaching."

"So what?"

"My guess, and it's only that, is that Eunice convinced Anna Jean that some of what your dad had should be hers. Plus, Anna Jean worked part-time in a bank. Maybe when she learned who he was, she figured out he had money."

"Dad would've…helped her if she needed it. Don't you think?"

Digger nodded. "I expect." She remembered his letter. He didn't say she had to show it to Franklin. Should she? "He'd probably have wanted more proof, not just the lawyer's letter."

"And what, this Anna Jean wandered around the house looking for stuff after Dad died?"

"I didn't listen to the sheriff deputies talking to them. Before he left with them, Charlie said Anna Jean took your dad's truck keys, which had a house key on the same ring. She said she put them back, which is why they had to break in here later, after I told Anna Jean I was going to Frostburg for a while." Digger grinned briefly. "And Eunice wanted some brooch."

Neither of them said anything for almost a minute.

Franklin stood and walked to the dining room and back. He returned with a tulip and gave it to Digger. "A get well present for your head."

She smiled and took it. "Thanks."

"And," he reached into a pocket and pulled out two letter-sized envelopes. "These were in Dad's box. One for me, one for you."

She took hers. "You, uh, mentioned the deed was there. I wondered what else."

"Mostly stuff of Mom's. I think he was guarding it." He opened his envelope and pulled out a caramel-colored brooch with a cream-colored, raised woman's profile. "I guess this is the brooch."

Digger opened her envelope, which was still sealed, and pulled out a small locket. She turned it over and handed it to Franklin. "Recognize it?"

He took it. "Kind of. I think I might have even broken the chain — accidentally — when I was really little. At least, I recall a story about that." He gave it back to Digger.

She opened it with the edge of a fingernail, bringing her face-to-face with tiny photos of an infant and a boy of perhaps one. She handed it to Franklin.

He stared at it for several seconds. "Guess I was so special she wanted two pictures of me close to her heart."

"Yeah, right." Digger took it back and studied the photos more closely. The infant on the left wasn't Franklin, she was sure of it. Was it Anna Jean? She started to say something, but changed her mind.

Franklin rubbed one eye. "I hope they keep that Damion in jail until some kind of trial, or he confesses."

"You think he'd come back here to hurt us?"

"I might hurt him."

"I can relate." Digger glanced around the kitchen, taking in the smudges left by the fingerprint team. "Lots of goop to clean up."

"I'd say it's your place so you have to do it, but you have a headache, so I'll start."

Franklin filled the sink with hot water and a lot of dishwashing detergent, then wet a sponge and tackled the black residue. The smudges came off, but some left a sort of shadow.

She figured she'd have a lot of repainting to do. "You don't have to move all your stuff out, you know."

"Franklin kept working, but nodded toward the upstairs and winked. "Maybe you and Marty will fill the bedrooms."

She rolled her eyes. "I barely know the guy."

"I can tell he likes you."

"A lot of people do. I'm serious. Leave stuff in your room."

He kept working, but eventually spoke. "I'll tell you what. I'll pay to build out the attic, and I'll make a mini apartment in part of it. Then if I come up on weekends, I won't interrupt your antics."

"Franklin!"

He grinned.

"Okay, good idea. But I'll pay."

"Nope. I want it done the way I want. And," he raised the sponge so Digger wouldn't interrupt him, "you're on unemployment, or will be, and the money Dad put aside for maintenance on this place will only cover it in years when something major doesn't break."

"I'll think about it."

Paws clambered down the steps from the second floor and Bitsy, accompanied by Ragdoll whose tiny paws made no noise, came to the kitchen doorway.

"I totally appreciate all you guys did, but if I give you any more treats you'll both be fat and sassy."

Ragdoll came over, sniffed her hand as Digger petted her, and jumped on the kitchen table. Bitsy settled at Digger's feet.

Digger sniffed the air. The familiar Uncle Benjamin smell had faded. The Ancestral Sanctuary's new owner had a lot of work to do.

CHAPTER TWENTY-EIGHT

THE SATURDAY FUNERAL AND following reception at the house weren't nearly as hard as Digger imagined they would be. Only Sheriff Montgomery and Marty Hofstedder had much of a clue about the activity the night before.

No one commented on Damion's absence. Few of Uncle Benjamin's friends knew they had dated, much less stopped. And with the lack of a daily paper, his arrest wasn't well known.

Digger carried an empty bowl into the kitchen, meaning to refill it with crackers, and Mrs. Zorn followed.

"You doing okay, Mrs. Zorn?"

"Thelma, please." She softly sang, "Oh when the saints come marching in."

Digger grinned. "As long as you don't call me Beth."

Thelma nodded. "Like that ex-boyfriend of yours."

Her smile faded.

Thelma squeezed her shoulder. "Mrs. Wilson, Marty's grandmother, told me about last night. She said some of it was also on a Pittsburgh television station, but I don't watch much."

"Oh. Thanks for not bringing it up in there." Digger nodded her head toward the living room.

Thelma shook her head. "Eunice was really broken up when Clara decided to give up that baby."

The cork from a bottle of champagne used to toast Uncle Benjamin rolled off the kitchen counter and Digger stooped to retrieve it. "So, you knew? I could have asked you?"

Thelma shrugged. "Why would you think I did? But I'm the same age as Eunice, and she and I both lived in Frostburg that summer. We didn't talk about it when I ran into them a couple of times, but it was obvious Clara was staying with her sister rather than at home. For a good reason."

Digger put the cork back on the counter and leaned against it. She almost whispered, "So why didn't Clara give the baby to Eunice?"

Thelma unwrapped the second of her pound cakes and placed it, already sliced, on a plate she took from the cupboard. "Eunice and Clara cared about each other, but Eunice was as sharp-tonged then as now. I don't know, but I guess Clara didn't want her baby to grow up hearing that. And perhaps if Eunice raised the child, it would have been too close a reminder of Clara's decision."

Digger nodded slowly. "I suppose...It's just so ironic. If Anna Jean had found us--Uncle Benjamin--first, it might have been different."

Thelma shrugged. "Maybe. I guess Eunice saw her niece, in part, as a way to get back at Benjamin rather than a chance to form a relationship, however late in life."

Franklin came into the kitchen and heard the last statement. "The whole thing's crazy." He nodded at Digger. "Couple people are telling the story about the time Dad set up Halloween decorations at the hardware store and scared the cr...daylights out of everyone when the witch called out their names."

"I was four. Scared me, too." Digger smiled. "I'll be right out." She pointed to the plate of pound cake. "Would you mind, Mrs...I mean, Thelma?"

Franklin walked back to the living room with Mrs. Zorn -- it would be a long time before Digger could think of her as Thelma -- and Digger rinsed her hands in the sink. Then she splashed cool water on her eyes, which still stung from shed and unshed tears.

The cork rolled off the counter and Digger again stooped to retrieve it. "Great. Maybe I need to get the foundation leveled."

"No, I'm just fooling with you."

She turned quickly and blinked rapidly. A faded, almost see-through, version of Uncle Benjamin sat cross-legged on the kitchen table.

"As soon as they put the last shovel of dirt over me I kind of popped out. Sat right on top of your aunt's headstone. Guess it's mine now, too."

Digger walked to the fridge, removed a bottle of jug wine, and twisted off the cap. She took a swig without bothering with a glass. Then she looked back at the table.

Uncle Benjamin grinned. "Didn't know you drank much."

"I'm starting."

"Probably not a bad idea."

THE END

ABOUT THE AUTHOR

Elaine L. Orr writes four mystery series, including the thirteen-book Jolie Gentil cozy mystery series, set at the Jersey shore. Two of her books (including *Behind the Walls* in the Jolie series) have been finalists for the Chanticleer Mystery and Mayhem Awards.

Unscheduled Murder Trip, second in the Family History Mystery Series, received an Indie B.R.A.G Medallion. Other books are in the River's Edge Series (set in rural Iowa) and the Logland Series (set in small-town Illinois).

She also writes plays and novellas. A member of Sisters in Crime, Elaine grew up in Maryland and moved to the Midwest in 1994. She enjoys meeting readers at events throughout the country.

Scan this QR code to visit my Author Page.

www.amazon.com/stores/Elaine-L.-Orr/author/B001HD0X6K

Authors always appreciate reviews. If you enjoyed *Least Trodden Ground*, please post a review on your favorite web site or mention it on Instagram or Facebook, Let your local bookstore or library know that you liked a book. You can also contact Elaine to see if she would be available in person or via Zoom to talk to your community or book group.

Scan this QR code to leave a review on Amazon.com

Amazon.com/review/create-review?&asin=B08KFLX6NG

www.elaineorr.com | www.elaineorr.blogspot.com
elaineorr55@yahoo.com

Printed in Great Britain
by Amazon